THE GUNSMITH

480

The Friendly Gold Mine

**Books by J.R. Roberts
(Robert J. Randisi)**

The Gunsmith series

Gunsmith Giant series

Lady Gunsmith series

Angel Eyes series

Tracker series

Mountain Jack Pike series

**COMING SOON!
The Gunsmith**
481 – Cheap Whiskey and Sad Women

**For more information
visit:** www.SpeakingVolumes.us

THE GUNSMITH

480

The Friendly Gold Mine

J. R. Roberts

SPEAKING VOLUMES, LLC
NAPLES, FLORIDA
2022

The Friendly Gold Mine

ISBN 978-1-64540-865-9

Chapter One

Denver, Colorado

Clint Adams had been to Denver many times, to see his friend, the private detective Talbot Roper. Often, it was just a friendly visit. Other times he had needed his friend's help or the other way around. This time he was there in response to a cryptic telegram that asked him to come to Denver for something different.

So Clint arrived in town out of curiosity.

As usual he left his Tobiano behind, this time with his friend John Locke, in Las Vegas, New Mexico, so he could take a train to Denver. From the train station he took a horse drawn cab to The Denver House Hotel, his home when he was in town.

"Mr. Adams," the clerk greeted him, "so nice to have you back with us."

He was greeted this way no matter who the clerk on the desk was, so he never managed to remember their names.

"Thank you very much."

The clerk handed him a key. "Your usual room. Do you need help with your luggage?"

"No, thanks," Clint said. "I have just one bag." He picked up his carpetbag. When he came to Denver, he usually needed more than he could carry in saddlebags.

"Then I'm sure you know the way, sir. Would you like a table this evening in the dining room?"

"Yes, I would. I'll freshen up and be down in half an hour."

"Your table will be ready."

Clint didn't know when he would be seeing Roper, but he was hungry now. He took his bag to his room on the second floor, and used the hotel's indoor, modern plumbing to clean up. When he came back down, he was greeted at the dining room door by a tuxedoed, middle-aged maître d' he remembered.

"Good evening, Mr. Adams," he said. "Your usual table?"

"Yes, James," he said, remembering the man's name.

"This way, sir," James said. "Your guest is already here."

"My guest?"

"Yes, sir."

He followed James across the floor, and, as they approached his table, he saw Talbot Roper already seated there.

"You sonofagun," Clint said, as they shook hands. "How'd you know I'd be here now?"

"I made arrangements," Roper said. "I wanted to talk to you as soon as you got here."

They sat across from each other.

"You must be hungry," Roper said, "so let's order first. This meal's on me."

"Two steaks, James," Clint said.

"I'll have your waiter bring them over, sir."

Roper already had a bottle of wine and two glasses on the table, but Clint said, "And bring me a beer with the meal."

"As you wish, sir," James said.

When the man walked away, Roper poured wine into their glasses.

He held his glass up and said, "I'm glad you're here. I have a proposition for you."

"It's about time you made me a partner in your agency," Clint said. "I'll even take second billing." He held his own glass up. "Roper and Adams."

"You're not far off from the truth," Roper said.

"Really?" Clint said, "I was kidding."

"Well, I'm not," Roper said. "I want you to be my partner."

"But not in your detective agency."

"No."

Clint sipped his wine, then put his glass down and sat back in his chair. He had no intention of picking it up again. The other diners who crowded the place, including some who were waiting for tables, found the two men interesting. Some of them even knew who Talbot Roper was.

"What's on your mind, Tal?" Clint asked.

"Nelson, Nevada," Roper said.

"What's in Nelson, Nevada?"

"You probably haven't heard about this, since it's fairly new," Roper said. "But . . . gold."

"Tal—" Clint started to chide his friend.

"Hear me out, Clint," Roper said. "This is a legitimate strike."

"I'm sure it is," Clint said. "But since when are you interested in mining gold?"

"Since now," Roper said. "I have a piece of a mine, there, but before I invest wholeheartedly, I need someone to check it out for me. Someone with experience."

"Ah," Clint said, "and there it is. If I check it out and it turns out to be a big strike, you'll make me a partner."

"Definitely."

"But don't you already have a partner who's already there?"

"Yes."

"And how does he feel about bringing me in?"

"He doesn't know, yet."

"And is he experienced?"

4

"At prospecting, yes," Roper said, "at operating a mine, no. But you are."

"Once or twice," Clint admitted.

"Well, let me tell you something about the Friendly Mine."

As the waiter approached with their plates Clint said. "How about over dinner?"

Chapter Two

"My partner's name is Pick-Axe Jones."

"Really?"

"Hear me out," Roper said. "He's been prospecting for forty years, and this is the first time he thinks he's found something."

"In forty years?" Clint said. "Nobody can say he didn't stick with it. How do you know him?"

"I met him on a case a few years back," Roper said. "He was a big help to me, and we kept in touch."

"And when did you hear from him about this?"

"He got in touch with me a couple of weeks ago, before the strike ever hit the newspapers. People are flocking there now, but Pick-Axe had filed his claim."

"Why does he need you?"

"He needs backing," Roper said. "He doesn't have money to set up the mining operation."

"And you want me to take a look at it before you commit fully to it."

"Exactly," Roper said. "I'll be committing the financing. I won't be able to work a gold claim and run my office."

"What if the gold strike is huge?" Clint asked. "If you become rich, would you still work?"

"I'll always work," Roper said. "I love being a detective. But I could expand and hire more men."

"Or women," Clint added.

"True," Roper said. "I never thought the Pinkertons would hire women, but they have."

"Coffee, gentlemen?" the waiter asked, as he cleared away the dishes.

"Bring Mr. Adams some peach pie," Roper said.

"Yes, sir."

"Wow," Clint said, "you're going all out."

"I'm just asking you to go and have a look, Clint," Roper said.

"And what about you?"

"I'll go with you," Roper said. "Between you, me and Pick-Axe we'll figure it out."

"And if it's a bust?"

"Pick-Axe will be used to that," Roper said, "and we'll go back to our lives. So where's the harm?"

"We'll have to get outfitted even to have a look, Tal," Clint said. "It could cost you a pretty penny."

"Hey, I've had a good year—a good few years, actually. I'm willing to invest."

Clint sat back while the waiter set down the pie. The man brought Roper a slice of apple—then poured the coffee and withdrew.

"This doesn't sound like you, Tal," Clint said. "You're a city man. This is going to be a gold mine in the mountains."

"I know that," Roper said. "I think I'm ready to try something different."

"What about your office?"

"I'll close it for a short time."

"And your cases?"

"I have none at the moment," Roper told him. "I wanted to be free and clear to do this."

"And if I say no?"

"I'll go on my own," Roper said. "No hard feelings. Pick-Axe and I will try to go it alone."

"Why not take a third partner?"

"That's what I'm trying to do," the detective said. "To tell the truth, I wouldn't trust anyone else but you."

Clint knew Roper wouldn't hold it against him if he said no, but if this mine was a bust, it could take a long while for Roper to figure it out. By the time he came back to Denver, his business could be ruined. There were plenty of other detective agencies who would be willing to take his business, including the Pinkertons. Clint knew Heck Thomas was out there, as well as Harry Morse, and even Virgil Earp had opened a detective agency. Roper was the best, but if he stayed away too long, people might forget and move on.

"You think I'm being foolish," Roper said. "I can see it on your face."

"Hey, your life is to do with what you want," Clint said. "I just wouldn't want to see you throw away all the success you've had."

"All the more reason you should come with me, to see that I don't waste any time."

Clint ate his last bite of pie and sat back.

"If you don't want to be a partner, I'll pay for your time as a consultant."

"Don't be stupid," Clint said. "I'm not trying to get money out of you."

"I know, I know," Roper said. "I'm sorry. Look, I'd just like to do this with someone I like and trust. It's enough I'll be digging in the ground, I don't want to also be looking over my shoulder."

Oh crap, Clint thought, I'm going to do this, ain't I.

"I tell you what," Roper said. "Think it over, don't decide now. I'm planning on leaving in two days. Just let me know by then."

That sounded fair.

"Okay," Clint said, "two days."

Roper grinned.

"Come on, let's go get a drink."

Chapter Three

Clint woke the next morning with a smooth, warm hip pressed to his. He turned his head to take a look, hoping against hope it wasn't Talbot Roper . . .

***

He and Roper had gone across the lobby to the Denver House's green-and-gold bar. They started with beer and then, at Roper's insistence, switched to whiskey. In the midst of their drinking, two couples entered the bar and sat at a table. The women were well-dressed and pretty, one blonde, one dark-haired. The men they were with appeared to be businessmen and immediately showed themselves to be arrogant assholes. They berated the bartender from the moment they entered, and then, when the women tried to quiet them, turned their ire on the ladies.

That was when Clint and Roper stepped in. They both rose and walked to the couples' table.

"You fellas want to keep it down?" Roper said.

"Who the hell're you?" one man demanded.

"I'm the man who's going to teach you a lesson if you continue being loud and mistreating these lovely ladies."

The other man looked at Clint and asked, "And you?"

"I'm going to help him," Clint said, taking a moment to smile at the ladies.

"You see," the dark-haired lady said to the first man, "I told you to quiet down."

"You shut the hell up, bitch!" the man said.

"That's it," the blonde said. "Let's go, Jennifer."

"Where do ya think you're goin'?" the second man demanded.

"We're leaving," she said. "You've become boring."

"Why you bitch!" the man swore and drew his hand back to strike her.

Clint stepped in and punched the man in the jaw knocking him and his chair over backward.

"Hey, who do you—" the other man started, but Roper cut him off by knocking him out with one punch.

"Would you ladies like to go somewhere more quiet?" Clint asked the women.

"We would love to," the blonde said.

She linked her arm in Clint's while the other woman did the same with Roper, and they all walked out, leaving the two men sprawled on the floor.

Clint recalled the pleased bartender wishing them all a good night . . .

***

Luckily, the hip pressed to his belonged to the blonde, whose name was Lacy Rose.

He rolled over, rested his head on his hand, to take a good look at her. Last night was fuzzy, but he remembered her being pretty, fairly smart, and perhaps thirty years old. Now, watching her while she slept, her face in repose, lost some of the years he'd given her the night before, and he figured she was perhaps twenty-six or seven.

Slowly, her eyelids fluttered and opened. When she saw him watching her, she smiled.

"I could feel your eyes on me," she said. "They woke me up."

"That's good," he said. "In a minute I was going to use my hands for that."

"Really?" She folded her hands beneath her chin and stared at him. "That sounds interesting. How would that work?"

"Well," he said, "you'd put your head back on the pillow, and I'd run my fingers along the line of your lovely back to your beautiful bum, and then squeeze."

As he squeezed one ass cheek, she moaned and closed her eyes.

"That's nice," she said. "What else?"

"Well," he said, "then I'd lean over and do the same thing with my tongue."

She moaned again, but then her eyes went wide, and she lifted her head to look around.

"Where's Jennifer?" She sounded worried.

"She's fine," Clint said. "She went home with Tal."

"Tal?"

"My friend, Talbot Roper."

Her face relaxed.

"Oh, the private detective?"

"That's right."

"How did she go home with him, and I come here with you?" she asked.

"I believe that was a choice you two girls made for yourselves."

"Oh, I remember," she said. "You're Clint Adams."

"Right."

"The Gunsmith."

"Right, again."

"You're both famous," she observed. "Handsome and famous."

"And you're both lovely," Clint said. "Seems to me you each made a good decision."

"From what I can remember, that seems true."

"Well," he said, kissing one of her plump cheeks, "I could continue to remind you."

"Oh," she said, putting her head back on the pillow, "please do."

Chapter Four

Clint ran his tongue down the girl's lovely back again, to her ass cheeks, nibbled on them a while, then turned her over and dove between her legs, face first. He worked her to a fever pitch with his tongue, enjoying the flavor of her nectar as it covered his face. She couldn't keep her legs still as the pleasure flowed through her, and in the end, she was beating her fists and heels on the mattress as she fought the urge to scream . . .

***

Too exhausted to speak, she caught her breath while dressing, then did the best she could arranging her long hair.

"How long will you be in town?" she asked.

"Probably only another day or two," he said.

Having straightened herself out the best she could, she turned to face him and said, "I don't know if I can get free again that soon."

"It's probably best," he said. "We really don't seem to have much time to spend together."

She smoothed down the front of her yellow dress and said, "Well, I think what we had last night was very nice."

"I agree."

She walked to the bed, ran her hand down his chest and kissed him.

"Thank you for a very pleasant evening, Mr. Adams," she said, "and a lovely morning."

"It was my pleasure, Lacy Rose."

She went out the door and paused to throw him one last kiss.

Clint lay with his hands behind his head, feeling a bit worn out after an energetic night with the lovely blonde. Then he suddenly remembered he was to meet Roper for breakfast. He quickly left the bed, refreshed himself in the indoor water closet, then dressed. He rarely wore his holster while in Denver but donned a jacket so no one could see the Colt New Line he tucked into his belt at the small of his back. Properly dressed, he left the room and went down to meet Roper in the dining room.

***

When he entered the dining room, he was surprised to see Roper already there. He must have had as rigorous

16

a night with Jennifer as Clint had with Lacy Rose. Maybe he had recovered more quickly than Clint had.

"How was your night?" Clint asked.

"Uneventful," Roper said. "The lady had to go home to her husband."

"What?"

"So, I guess, between the two of us, you were the one who got lucky."

Clint sat across from his friend.

"Was Lacy also married?" Roper asked.

"That never came up with us," Clint said.

"Would it have bothered you?" Roper asked.

Clint thought a moment, then said, "To tell you the truth, I don't know. I don't make a habit of sleeping with married women, but it turned out to be quite a night."

"So, I guess you didn't have time to think about my proposal."

"Actually, I didn't," Clint said, "but I don't really need to, Tal. I'll come along with you."

Roper's face lit up.

"That's great! This calls for a big celebratory breakfast—on me, of course.

"Sounds good," Clint said.

The waiter came over and they ordered.

"When do we leave?" Clint asked.

"I've got two tickets for an early train tomorrow morning," Roper said.

"Am I that predictable?"

"Not really," Roper said. "I could've bought them for today."

***

They ate breakfast with Clint telling Roper about his few experiences with gold mines.

"You may call that a few," Roper said, "but it's a helluva lot more than I've had. The important thing is that now I have a partner I can trust."

"If we're partners," Clint said, "I want to share in backing the venture."

"That's not necessary," Roper said, "but we can deal with that when we get there. We'll have to outfit when we get off the train, and then load up a wagon for the rest of the trip."

"How long will we be riding the trail in a wagon?" Clint asked.

"It's about a hundred and fifteen miles from Linville to Nelson, and another ten or so to the mine site."

Clint finished his breakfast, wishing he had thought to bring the Tobiano along.

Chapter Five

Pick-Axe Jones checked in with the telegraph office in Nelson. There was really no operator there, but because of the strike, they had arranged for a rider to bring telegrams from Linville a couple of times a week.

He passed a few new saloons that had been erected since he last came to town. The word had not yet spread about the gold strike near Nelson, but as soon as it did, this would become a boom town, with more claims being filed, new businesses springing up, and pickpockets, bushwhackers and whores staking their own kinds of claims.

A lot of the girls would work out of the new saloons being opened, but many of them would ply their trade from tents at a nickel a poke.

"Anythin' for me, Ezra?" Pick-Axe asked as he entered the telegraph tent.

"You bet, Pick-Axe," Ezra Kotzwinkle said. "Here ya go, from Denver."

"Thanks."

Pick-Axe took the telegram and stepped outside the tent. It had three words: ON THE WAY. That suited Pick-Axe just fine. He couldn't wait for Talbot Roper to arrive so they could get started digging that color out of the ground.

He tucked the telegram into his pocket and headed for one of the new saloons. He had a nickel and had decided to spend it on beer, not a whore.

***

"There he goes," Tucker Samuels said.

"He's headin' for a saloon," his partner, Ike Milligan said. "We gonna kill 'im today?"

"How many times I gotta tell ya?" Samuels asked him. "We can't kill 'im until we know where his claim is."

"And when are we gonna know that?"

"He's cagey," Samuels said. "He's been at this for a long time. He's smarter than to let people know where he's staked his claim."

"If he's been at it a long time, why ain't he ever hit it rich?" Milligan asked.

"He ain't been lucky," Samuels said. "But I've known him long enough to know that he can tell when there's color in the ground."

"So whatta we do?"

"Let's go and buy the man a drink," Samuels said, and they followed Pick-Axe.

***

Clint met Roper at the train station the next morning.

"Quiet night?" Roper asked, after they had boarded and found seats.

"Quieter and more restful than last night," Clint confirmed.

"Just as well," Roper said. "We need to be in good shape for what's coming."

"You're right," Clint said. "Mining is hard work. You said this partner of yours has been at it a while. Just how old is he?"

"Hmm, that's a good question," Roper said. "He's kind of small, looks like he's made of gristle. He must be more than sixty."

"Then he *has* been at it a long time," Clint said. "I hope he's in shape for this."

"Oh, don't worry about Pick-Axe," Roper said. "He takes care of himself."

"Does he drink?"

"Not when he's working."

"Whores?"

"Again, not when he's working."

"And he knows his business?"

"He says he can smell color in the ground," Roper said. "He just hasn't been lucky enough to hit it big—maybe until now."

"He's had some success?"

"He says he's had a few good hits, but he didn't have the financial backing to get it out of the ground. He's sold a couple of claims over the years that other people have turned into something."

"Outright?" Clint asked. "Why not keep a piece."

"Clint, Pick-Axe has one problem."

"What's that?"

"He can be conned."

"After all these years?" Clint asked.

"He's a bit of a pushover," Roper said. "That's one reason he contacted me to be his partner. He knows I'll keep him from making mistakes."

"We just have to get there before he makes one, right?" Clint asked.

"That's right."

"And he knows we're coming?"

"I sent a telegram," Roper said. "He just has to stay out of trouble until we get there."

"Honestly," Clint asked, "what are the chances of that?"

"In the past I would have said slim," Roper admitted, "but this time he thinks he's really found it."

Chapter Six

They felt some aches from sleeping in their seats when they reached Linville, but they went to a livery stable to rent a buckboard. Because buckboards were in demand, the cost was five times what it might usually have been, but they needed it to transport the supplies they were bringing to the Friendly Gold Mine.

"I don't have one," the hostler said, irately. "There ain't any kind of wagon in town. If I had more, I could rent 'em all in one day."

"Are you getting any more?" Roper asked.

"I hope so," the man said. "I sent for 'em."

"When should they get here?" Clint asked.

"Hopefully a day or two," the big man said.

"Well, we want one," Roper said.

"I got six comin', but they're all spoke for."

"And how soon will you get more after that?" Clint asked.

"Probably a week."

Clint and Roper exchanged a glance.

"That's too long," Roper said. "I don't think Pick-Axe can stay out of trouble that long."

"What are you not telling me?" Clint asked.

"I told you he didn't drink while he was working," Roper said. "Well, he's not working now, he's just waiting for us."

"So he could get drunk and do something stupid."

"Yes."

Clint turned to the hostler. "What's your name?"

"Arnold."

"Well, Arnold, we need the first buckboard that you get tomorrow."

"I hope I'm gettin' 'em tomorrow."

"It should be in the next couple of days, right?" Clint asked.

"Hopefully," Arnold said, "but like I said, they're all spoke for."

"We'll pay you double," Roper said. He looked at Clint. "I'll have to take you up on your offer to help with money."

"You got it," Clint said. He looked at Arnold. "Is there a bank in town?"

"Yeah," Arnold said, "two of 'em. But . . . double? I gotta tell ya, I already raised my prices five times. And I got customers—"

"We're customers," Clint said. "This is Talbot Roper, and my name's Clint Adams."

Arnold looked startled.

"Adams?" he repeated. "The Gunsmith?"

"That's right," Clint said. "And I need a buckboard."

"Y-yessir," Arnold said. "You'll h-have the first one I g-get. Yessir."

"Thanks, Arnold," Clint said. "Thanks a lot. We better get a hotel room."

"You won't find one," Arnold said. "The town's full, but you can stay in here, if you want. Up in the hayloft. No charge."

"Thanks, Arnold," Clint said. "We'll take that offer." He looked at Roper. "Let's get a meal and a beer."

"Sounds good. We can also pick up some supplies."

"You better hurry," Arnold said. "Those are goin' fast, too. Um, if you tell 'em your name . . ."

"Yes, yes," Clint said, "I know."

Clint and Roper left the livery.

"You're not happy," Roper said. "I know you don't like using your name that way."

"No, I don't," Clint said. "It makes me out to be a bully."

"Well," Roper said, "let's see if we can get some supplies without using it."

***

They stopped at a large general store which seemed to have every piece of equipment they would need to mine the gold. They picked out shovels, pickaxes, and wood to build a sluice, as well as a tent to erect as shelter.

"A lot of this equipment is already spoke for, gents," the owner said. "I can getcha more, but it'll take time."

"We don't have time—" Roper started, but was interrupted when a harried looking man ran in.

"Excuse me," the owner said.

He went to talk with the man and seemed startled by something he was told. He looked over at Clint and Roper, then said something to the man, who left. The owner came back over.

"I'll have you gents' supplies ready whenever you like," he said.

"Well," Roper said, "as soon as we get a buckboard."

"That's fine. Just let me know. I'll have it stockpiled in the back til then."

"Thank you," Roper said. "How much do I owe you?"

"I'll let you know when you pick the stuff up."

"Thank you," Roper said, again.

He and Clint stepped outside and seemed to become the center of attention on the crowded street.

"I guess the word's out," Roper said.

"And because of that," Clint said, "I might be more trouble than I'm worth."

Chapter Seven

Clint and Roper got a table in a small café and settled for a couple of bowls of beef stew.

"When do we meet up with Pick-Axe?" Clint asked.

"For that we have to get to Nelson," Roper said. "And we need our buckboard for that trip."

"And when we get to Nelson?" Clint said. "We continue on to the mine?"

"Well, that's a problem," Roper said.

"How so?"

"I don't know where the mine is," Roper said. "Nobody but Pick-Axe does."

"He must have filed his claim," Clint said. "That means somebody in the claim office knows."

"He hasn't filed it, yet," Roper said. "I got a telegram saying he was afraid to, until I got here."

"So we came all this way and don't know where the mine is," Clint said, "or if he even still has it."

"His telegram assured me that no one would find it."

"*He* found it," Clint pointed out.

"By accident," Roper said.

"Then somebody else could find it, by accident."

"Hopefully not."

"Well, so far we've got our buckboard and our supplies. So the next thing is to find Pick-Axe and the mine."

"I'm sure we'll find Pick-Axe in Nelson. And he'll take us to the mine."

"And how's he going to feel about me coming along?" Clint asked.

"He trusts me, and I trust you. It'll be fine."

***

They spent the night in the livery stable hayloft, but it was not uneventful.

Arnold, the hostler, had supplied them with an oil lamp, which they extinguished when they were ready to go to sleep. No sooner had they done that and closed their eyes, they heard something below them.

Roper reached out and touched Clint.

"I hear it," Clint whispered.

Their eyes were used to the dark, so they could see one another. Clint waved at Roper to roll to one side of the loft, while he rolled to the other.

The sound of shots inside the livery were deafening. Lead punched up through the floor where they had been lying moments before.

Clint and Roper both rolled to the edge of the loft, and off. When they hit the floor, their guns were in their hands. They startled the two shooters, but the men still had their guns in their hands, so Clint and Roper were met with no choice. The two men fired in panic, while Clint and Roper coolly fired one shot each.

It grew quiet and Clint said, "I'll light a lamp."

He crossed the room to a lamp that hung on a post. As the yellow light bathed the room, both men walked to the dead.

"Know them?" Clint asked.

"No, never saw them before."

"Even here in town during the day?"

"Never. You think Arnold set us up by letting us stay here?" Roper asked.

"We know the word got out that we're here. We can ask him about it in the morning," Clint said. "Well, one of us better get the law and let them know what happened here. One of us should stay here."

"I'll stay," Roper said. "You might as well let the law know who you are, right away."

"I'll be back soon."

"Watch your back," Roper said.

"You, too."

Chapter Eight

Clint found a sheriff's office a few streets away. It was dark, and when he tried the door, he found it locked. He knocked, thinking the lawman might be asleep inside, but there was no answer. The man might have decided to try a saloon or two before going home. And someone there might know where he lived.

The second saloon he tried was called The Linville House Saloon, and he found a man with a badge standing at the bar. When he got closer, he saw that it was a sheriff's badge.

"Sheriff," he said, approaching the man.

"Yes, sir?" The man looked at him, "Can I help you?"

He was in his forties and had the bearing of a man who had worn the iron on his chest for many years.

"My name's Clint Adams. Someone just tried to kill my friend and me."

"Where'd this happen?"

"In the livery stable owned by a man named Arnold."

The sheriff gave a wistful look to the beer on the bar before him, then said, "You better tell me about it on the way."

***

When Clint entered the livery with the sheriff, he made the introductions.

"Sheriff Winter, this is Talbot Roper."

"I've heard of you, Mr. Roper," Winter said. "Both of you. What are you doin' here?"

"We're considering buying into a mine," Roper said.

"I see," the sheriff said, looking down at the two dead men.

"Do you know them, Sheriff?"

"I've seen them," Winter admitted, "but I don't know them."

He walked over and stood beneath the hayloft, looking up at the holes.

"They certainly tried to murder you in your sleep," he observed.

"Yes, sir," Roper said, "they did that."

Winter looked around, then asked. "Do you think Arnold was involved? After all, this is his stable."

"I thought we'd ask him that in the morning," Clint said.

"We'll do that together, if you don't mind," the lawman said.

"That's fine with us," Clint said, and Roper nodded.

"Would you like me to find you another place to stay?" Winter asked.

"No, this is fine," Clint said.

"Then I'll have these bodies removed and you can get some sleep."

"We thank you," Roper said.

"If you'd both come to my office in the morning, I'd appreciate it."

"We'll be there," Clint said.

They stood aside while the sheriff had several men remove the bodies, and then went back to the hayloft for a fitful night's sleep.

***

As they entered the sheriff's office the next morning, the man asked, "Coffee?"

"Please," Clint said.

Sheriff Winter poured them each a cup, then sat behind his desk. The small office was crowded and, with no other chairs, Clint and Roper were forced to stand.

"I've identified the shooters," the lawman said. "It looks as if Arnold had nothin' to do with the shooting, although I haven't talked to him, yet."

"We were going to do that together," Clint reminded him.

"Right."

"So who were they?" Roper asked.

"One of the bartenders identified them as two strangers who rode in a couple of days ago. Looks like they heard you were in town and decided to give it a try."

"While we were asleep," Roper said. "I guess that's the best way."

"Well," Winter said, "I'm findin' that you two did what you had to do. You were justified in killin' them."

"Is that up to the sheriff around here?" Clint asked.

"And the Justice of the Peace," Winter said, "which I am, so yes, it's up to me." He stood up. "Let's go and talk to Arnold."

They followed him out of the office.

***

They found Arnold at the livery, and he seemed genuinely shocked to hear what had happened.

"I hope you don't think—"

"No, we don't, Arnold," the sheriff assured him. "They were a couple of drifters who decided to make a try for the Gunsmith."

"Damn," Arnold said, "they put some holes in my hayloft."

"Yeah," Clint said, "sorry about that."

"Ah," Arnold said, "it's not your fault."

"Anythin' else I can do for you fellas?" Sheriff Winter asked.

"We've got some business with Arnold," Roper said.

"I'll leave you to it, then," Winter said, and left.

"What about our buckboard?" Clint asked.

"They came in today," Arnold said, "I got three in the back. Take your pick."

He took them out back and they chose the sturdiest of the three.

"You'll need a team," Arnold said, pointing to his corral. "Pick out two."

They chose two eight-year-olds who had been hauling freight for a few years.

"I'll hook 'em up," Arnold said.

"We'll drive it over to the general store to pick up our goods, and then we'll get going," Roper said. "Won't take long."

Arnold hooked them up, then settled up with Clint and Roper, giving them what seemed like a good deal.

"Nice doing business with you, Arnold," Roper said.

"I'm sorry about the shootin'," Arnold said. "Guess I shoulda kept my mouth shut about you bein' in town, Mr. Adams. No hard feelin's?"

Clint shook the man's hand and said, "No hard feelings."

Chapter Nine

They drove the buckboard over to the general store and loaded their goods out of the back.

The owner helped them pack the buckboard, and then they went inside to settle up. Clint had made a stop at a Denver bank before boarding the train, so he had money to give Roper to assist in buying the goods.

When their business was done in Linville, they got directions to Nelson from the owner of the general store, then climbed aboard and rode out, with Clint driving the rig. They were prepared for at least a five-day trip if, they pushed.

Everything was tied down in the back of the buckboard, but several times during the trip, over rough terrain, the ropes came loose, and they had to stop to tie it all down again.

The third night they camped, they sat over the campfire and shared beans and coffee.

"I hope these delays haven't added too much time to the trip," Clint said.

"I'd say another day or so," Roper said. "When we get there, we'll find Pick-Axe."

Clint poured another cup of coffee and looked out into the darkness.

"Anything?" Roper asked.

"Hmm? Oh, no, I haven't felt anyone following us since we left town. Apparently, those two were the only ones who wanted to make a try for us."

"Us?" Roper said. "I think they were trying for you, my friend."

"You're probably right, which is why I said I might be more trouble than I'm worth on this venture."

"I'm willing to take a chance," Roper said. "I'll take the first watch."

They had set watches each night on the trail, just in case someone else was on their tail.

"Fine," Clint said, "Wake me in four hours."

Clint rolled himself up in his bedroll against the chill of the fall night and fell asleep.

***

He opened his eyes when the smell of fresh coffee tickled his nostrils and saw the cup Roper was holding beneath his nose.

"Thanks," he said, sitting up and accepting it.

"No sign of anyone and no sounds," Roper said, grabbing his own bedroll.

"I'll wake you in the morning with breakfast," Clint promised.

"Suits me," Roper said, and almost immediately fell asleep.

Clint took his coffee to the fire, stoked it a bit with more wood, then sat and drank, staring out into the dark.

He was hoping he hadn't made a mistake coming on the expedition. He certainly trusted Tal Roper, but this Pick-Axe fellow sounded like another matter. And yet Roper trusted the man. Well, he had already come this far, and had now invested more than just time, so there was no point in turning back.

Over the next four hours, he saw that Roper was right. There was no noise from out in the dark. He doubted anyone could be watching them without even making an unintentional sound of a foot scrape.

As first light bloomed, he tossed some bacon into a pan and put on a pot of fresh coffee. There was no point in waking Roper, as the combined scents did the job.

After breakfast they broke camp and moved on.

It took a few hours for an itch to form in the center of Clint's back.

"Somebody's behind us," he said to Roper, who was driving.

"How could they be behind us now and not the past three days?" Roper asked. "And they're not making a sound at night."

"Apparently," Clint said, "they're good at what they do."

"What do you want to do?" Roper asked.

"On the next bend in this road I'm going to jump off and wait to see who it is and what they want," Clint said.

"What they want's fairly obvious," Roper said. "Either you, or they're following us to the mine."

"If they want me," Clint said, "they're going to get me. If they want our mine, they're going to have to get their own."

About fifteen minutes later they saw a bend up ahead.

"Just slow down a bit, then keep going at normal speed," Clint said.

"You don't want me to stop up ahead?" Roper said.

"No," Clint said. "I'll catch up."

"On foot?"

Clint slapped Roper on the back.

"I'm sure whoever's following us will give me a horse."

Chapter Ten

Clint hid behind a rock and waited. For a few minutes he wondered if he was going to have to catch up to Talbot Roper on foot. Then he heard horses, moving not at a gallop, but a trot. They were following, but not trying to catch up at that point. He stayed crouched, perched on his toes. As two riders came into view, he sprang to his feet and jumped out in front of them, gun in hand.

"Stop right there!"

They reined in, one horse rearing up.

"Keep your hands away from your guns!"

They obeyed, one man after fighting for control of his horse.

"You tryin' to get me thrown?" the man demanded, "What the hell are you doin'?"

"I don't like being followed."

"What?" the other man said. "We ain't followin' you."

"Yeah, you are," Clint said. "Take your guns out with two fingers and toss them."

They did so.

"Now the rifles. Toss them to the same side."

They threw the rifles over by the pistols.

"Now step down and forward."

They dismounted and took a few steps forward. They were both in their forties, one slightly taller than the other.

"What are your names?"

"I'm Pete Krechmer," the slightly taller one said, "this is Jelly Buchanan."

"Now what's this about?" Clint said. "A chance at the Gunsmith?"

"What? Hell, no," Krechmer said, "there's no way we wanna face you with a gun."

"Those two in the livery stable didn't want to face me, either."

"We heard about that," Jelly said. "We ain't interested in you."

"Then why are you following us? Is it Roper?"

"We don't even know who he is," Krechmer said.

"Well, it's something," Clint said. "After our gold?"

The two men exchanged a look, and then Krechmer said, "We're lookin' for Pick-Axe Jones."

That surprised Clint.

"What makes you think we know him?"

"Somethin' you said in the saloon," Krechmer said. "The bartender heard it."

"Why are you interested in Pick-Axe?" Clint asked.

"We got business," Jelly said.

"He owes us," Krechmer said. "We intend to collect."

"That's your business with him," Clint said. "I don't want to get involved with that. Besides, I don't even know him, or where he is."

They exchanged another look.

"Your partners," Jelly said.

"Actually, I'm partners with Roper," Clint said, "and Roper's partners with Pick-Axe. So Roper and I have no business with you. Move away from your horses, and away from the guns."

They moved to the other side of the road. Clint walked to the horses, mounted one and picked up the lead off the other.

"You ain't gonna leave us out here on foot," Krechmer complained.

"Hey," Clint said, "I'm leaving you your guns. Be satisfied with that."

Clint started to ride away.

"Hey, Adams!" Krechmer shouted.

"What?" Clint answered without stopping.

"Tell Pick-Axe we'll be seein' him soon," the man called out.

Clint waved a hand, still without turning. He doubted the men would pick up their guns and start shooting, and he was right.

Chapter Eleven

When Clint caught up to Roper, the detective had stopped.

"I thought you were going to keep moving," Clint said, riding up alongside him.

"It was taking too long," Roper said. "I thought you might have to catch up to me on foot."

"I was thinking that too, but then these two came along."

"What did they want?"

"I'll tell you as we go."

Clint stayed on the horse and rode alongside the buckboard, telling Roper of his encounter with Krechmer and Jelly.

"Pick-Axe owes them . . . what?"

"That they didn't say," Clint replied. "They just said they'd collect."

"Well," Roper said, "Pick-Axe had lots of dealings with lots of men over the years. I'm sure he's made some enemies." He looked at the horse Clint was riding. "What do you want to do with these horses?"

"We'll take them with us," Clint said. "We might get some use out of extra animals."

"But they don't belong to us," Roper said.

"They do now."

"But we—"

"If it makes you feel better," Clint added, "we'll give them back at some point."

They camped one more night and made Nelson the next day.

***

The streets were packed with people and wagons, buildings had been hastily constructed, some of both wood and tarp. Others were in the act of being built, of newly cut wood.

It was stop and go just to get two streets before they arrived.

"How do we find Pick-Axe?" Clint asked.

"Let's try right here," Roper pointed. "He would have had to file his claim here."

They mounted the boardwalk, just barely missed being knocked down by miners rushing in and out. They finally entered the claim office, and waited in line to speak with the clerk.

When they reached the front Roper said, "I thought the word wasn't out, yet."

"It's out now," the clerk said. "Whataya got?"

"We're looking for Pick-Axe Jones," Roper said. "We're his partners in the Friendly Mine."

"I haven't seen Pick-Axe in days, maybe weeks," the man said.

"He sent me a telegram saying he was holding off on filing, afraid someone would steal his claim."

"That's true," the clerk said, "but when the word got out, I convinced him to file, or lose the claim, anyway."

"And when was that?"

"A couple of weeks, I think. And I haven't seen him since then. Did he know you were coming?"

"Yes," Roper said, "but he didn't know when. We hoped to be able to find him here."

"That'll take you some time," the clerk said. "And I doubt you'll find any place to stay."

"That won't be a problem," Clint said. "We're used to camping."

"If you fellas wouldn't mind," the clerk said, "I have quite a line of men waiting behind you to file their claims."

"One more question," Roper said.

"What's that?"

Roper leaned in and lowered his voice.

"Can you tell us where Pick-Axe's claim is?"

"Not right now, in front of all these people," the clerk said. "Come back after five."

"We'll see you then," Roper said.

He and Clint left the office and stood just outside.

Clint stopped a man walking by and asked him, "Where can we get a good steak?"

"A couple of streets that way," the man said. "The Torchlight Café."

"Thank you."

"You think our goods are safe here?" Roper asked.

Clint looked around and saw quite a few men eyeing the contents of their buckboard.

"Probably not. We should eat in shifts."

"You go first," Roper said. "I'll talk with some of these people and see if they know anything about Pick-Axe."

"I'll be back as fast as I can," Clint said.

"It's three," Roper said. "Get back by four, and then I can return by five."

"Right."

Clint started in search of the café.

***

The steak was edible, which was more than could be said about the vegetables. He warned Roper about it when he got back.

"You'd be better off with something easier to chew, like chicken."

"Thanks for the warning."

"Any information about Pick-Axe?"

"He's known by a lot of these people," Roper said, "but apparently respected by none."

"That's too bad. Nobody knows where he is? Or where his claim is?"

"No one."

"Well," Clint said, "when you get back, we'll see what the clerk in the claims office has to say."

"See you soon."

Chapter Twelve

Clint spoke to several men while he waited and got the same impression. They all seemed to know Pick-Axe, but nobody believed in him.

"If you're alignin' yourself with him," one man told him, "you're out of luck. I'd be glad to take these goods off your hands."

"That's okay," Clint said. "We'll hang onto them."

"Suit yourself."

Clint sat on the buckboard bench until he saw Roper approaching.

"How was it?" Clint asked, dropping to the ground.

"No better than you," Roper said, "but at least I'm not hungry anymore. How're we doing here?"

"I had an offer on our supplies."

"I hope you turned it down."

"What do you think?" Clint asked. "Let's get to that claim office. It looks like the clerk just closed it."

They knocked on the door several times before the clerk opened the door.

"I'm sorry, I was in the back," he said. "You wanted to know where Pick-Axe's claim was."

"That's right," Roper said. "We'll look for him there."

"How do you know Pick-Axe?" the clerk asked.

"We're friends," Roper said.

"How is Pick-Axe friends with you?"

"What's your name?" Roper asked.

"I'm Paul Weber."

"How do you know Pick-Axe?"

"We've been in on several strikes together," Weber said. "I've always been a claim clerk. Pick-Axe knows his business, but he's never been lucky. I hope he is this time."

"Well, my name's Roper, I'm a private detective from Denver. Pick-Axe helped me on a case a while back, and we became friends. When he needed a partner he could trust, he sent me a telegram."

"And your partner?" Weber asked, looking at Clint.

"This is Clint Adams."

Weber looked surprised.

"Pick-Axe is partners with the Gunsmith?"

"He's partners with Roper," Clint corrected. "I'm partners with Roper, as well."

"Is that enough?" Roper asked.

"I like Pick-Axe," Weber said. "I just don't want to get taken."

"Do you know where he is?" Clint asked.

"I don't," Weber said. "I'm hoping he's all right."

"He might be at his claim waiting for me," Roper said.

"We can all hope so," Weber said. "Here." He held out a folded piece of paper.

"What's this?"

"It's a map to the Friendly Mine," Weber said. "I assume you are the friends."

"We are," Roper said. "Thanks for this."

He and Clint walked to the door, which Weber unlocked.

"Do you have any idea how long it would take to get to this claim?"

"Hours," Weber said. "You're better off starting out there in the morning."

"Do you know of a place with a couple of beds?" Clint asked.

"Not in town," Weber said. "Rooms have already been doubled up."

"Anyplace with a barn that might be available?" Roper asked.

"You'd be sharing it," Weber said. "And you don't know with what kind of men. You're better off camping outside of town."

"That was our original plan," Roper said. "If you happen to see Pick-Axe, let him know we're waiting for him out at the mine."

"I'll do that." the clerk promised.

Clint and Roper stepped out of the office. Their buckboard loaded with goods had gone untouched while they were inside. They climbed aboard after tying the two horses to the back.

"We'll camp North of town, since that's the direction we'll be going tomorrow."

"Any sort of clearing will do," Clint said. "But we'll have to continue to keep watch."

"Agreed."

It took them a while to negotiate the crowded streets of Nelson, but they eventually got out of town. The road was a worn one, and they wanted to camp far enough from it to not be detected.

"Wait, what's that?" Clint asked, pointing.

Roper reined the team in.

"Looks like it might have been well-traveled at one time, but it's since overgrown," Roper observed.

"Let's try it," Clint said.

Roper started the team up again, turning onto the overgrown road. Clint turned and looked behind, saw that that dense foliage had stood back up after they passed. It would take days of traveling back and forth to make the road noticeable, and they only intended to travel it one more time, in the morning.

Chapter Thirteen

They found a clearing, unhitched the team and teth-ered all four horses to a line. After that they collected wood, started a fire, and put on a pot of coffee. While they drank it, Clint prepared a pan of bacon-and-beans.

Clint saw that Roper was deep in thought.

"You're worried about Pick-Axe," he said to the de-tective.

"Yes," Roper said. "Anything could've happened to him."

"If he's smart," Clint said, "He's hunkered down in his mine, waiting for you. That would've been the right thing to do after filing his claim."

"I hope that's where he is," Roper said. "I don't know how this would work without him."

"There's no point in worrying about it now," Clint said. "Let's deal with it when the time comes."

"You're right, of course."

"I'll take the first watch tonight," Clint said. "Get some sleep. We'll get an early start."

"Right you are," Roper said. He dumped the rem-nants from his cup and rolled himself up in his bedroll.

***

Clint woke Roper with a cup of coffee and said, "Get me up at first light and we'll get started."

"You got it," Roper said.

True to his word he woke Clint, also with a cup of coffee.

"You want breakfast?" he asked, at the same time.

"I'd just as soon get started following that map," Clint said.

"Suits me, too."

After dousing the fire, they finished their coffee and stowed the pot, then hitched up the team, and tied the other two horses—all saddled—to the back of the buckboard. They rode out of that hidden clearing to the main road and, keeping an eye behind them, started to follow Paul Weber's map.

After half a day, they still couldn't find the Friendly Mine, map or no map.

"Even with a map this place is hard to find," Clint said.

"If we trust that Weber was giving us the right information," Roper added. "We only have his word that he's friends with Pick-Axe."

"If it turns out something's happened to Pick-Axe, we'll have to press Weber," Clint said.

Clint looked over at Roper, who was staring at the map again.

"Hey Clint," Roper said, "I may be a dumb sonofa-bitch and holding this map the wrong way."

Clint took a look.

"Doesn't look like Weber bothered marking North from south."

"No, but he said we had to go north," Roper said. "So we're going in the right general direction."

Clint looked around.

"We haven't seen the markings of any other claims," he pointed out.

"Okay," Roper said, "so if I had the map upside down, we should have headed East back there, not West."

"Let's backtrack and see," Clint suggested.

Roper turned the team around and headed back the way they had come.

"There," Clint pointed. "That's a road."

Roper drove to the mouth of the road and reined in.

"Is it wide enough for us?" he wondered.

"If it's not, we'll be hauling these supplies up by hand," Clint said.

"Then let's give it a try," Roper said.

He snapped the reins at the team and got them moving up the slightly inclined road.

***

At one point, the incline got steeper, and Roper stopped.

"I've got an idea," he said.

"What is it?"

"Let's take those other two horses and leave the rig here, for now. If we're in the wrong place, there's no point in driving the team up."

"Well, it's pretty isolated here," Clint said. "I don't think we're going to lose our goods. Let's try it."

Roper put the brake on, and they climbed down. They walked to the two saddled horses, climbed aboard and urged them on up the incline.

It started to get pretty steep, and the horse's hooves began to slide in the rocky ground.

"We better walk them from here," Clint suggested.

"Or just leave them and go ahead on foot."

They dismounted, tied the horses off on some shrubbery and continued on foot.

When they came around a turn, they saw that the road ran straight into a rock wall.

"Well, hell," Roper said, "I thought we had it."

Chapter Fourteen

Clint and Roper stared at the bare rock wall.

"Now what?" Roper asked.

"Let's move around to either side," Clint said. "You go left, I'll go right. Sing out if you find anything."

"Right."

They moved apart, Clint followed the rock face wall to the right for about ten yards before he came to what looked like the mouth of a mine. He also heard water trickling, so he went a few more yards and found a stream that was being fed by water falling from above. It wasn't a full-on waterfall, but there was enough water for them to build a sluice. He was pretty certain he had found Pick-Axe's Friendly Mine.

"Talbot!" he shouted.

"Coming!"

Roper came trotting around from his side and stopped short when he saw the mine.

"This it?" he asked.

"Looks like it."

"Doesn't appear like he did a thing out here."

"Except build a fire, and that was a while ago," Clint said. "There's also a stream here we can use, but first we've got to make sure this is the right place."

"How do we do that?"

"We go inside and take a look."

"We'll need some tools," Roper said. "I'll have to go back to the buckboard."

"Wait," Clint said. "Let's go inside first and see what's what. Maybe Pick-Axe left some tools inside."

"Good idea."

They entered the mine, and the first thing they found was an oil lamp. Clint lit it, and they continued holding the lamp aloft.

The next thing they found on the ground was a pick-axe.

"There you go," Clint said. "That's what we need."

He handed the lamp to Roper and picked up the axe. They moved on.

They found a few wooden supports used to shore up the ceiling of the mine.

"It sure would be good to find Pick-Axe in here," Clint said.

"Yeah," Roper said. "Safe and sound."

They moved a little further before Clint said, "Stop!"

"What is it?"

"Look at the walls," Clint said. "Looks like Pick-Axe did some work here. Hold that lamp up."

Roper got close to the wall with the lamp and held it up. Clint started to pick away with the axe. It took only a few minutes for him to find what he wanted.

"See that?" he asked.

"What is it?"

"Color," Clint said, using a little more elbow grease on the axe. "There's a vein here."

"So it's a strike?" Roper asked.

"That depends on how deep the vein goes," Clint said, "and that's going to take some work to discover."

"But there's something here," Roper said.

"Oh, there's something here, all right," Clint said.

Roper got excited and almost dropped the lamp.

"Take it easy," Clint told him. "Let's go back outside."

They retraced their steps, extinguished the lamp and left it just inside, before stepping out.

"So we found it," Roper said.

"Unless we found somebody else's mine," Clint said. "We're going to have to find Pick-Axe to be sure."

"Well, according to the map, we found it," Roper pointed out.

"I'd feel better if we'd see a sign that said Friendly Mine."

"What do you want to do?" Roper asked.

"I don't want to start working in earnest until we know more," Clint said, "but there's no harm in trying to get the buckboard closer."

"I think the road widened a bit the higher we got," Roper said. "We should be able to do it."

"Well, let's go back down and start on that," Clint said.

"This was pretty hard to find," Roper said. "You really think somebody else found it?"

"We're going to find out."

***

Clint and Roper went back to the buckboard. Roper got into the seat, and Clint went to the front to give the team some encouragement.

The sides of the buckboard scraped against the sides of the rocks, and at one point one of the wheels slipped off the trail.

"Stop, before we break the wheel," Clint said and moved to the buckboard to check the wheel.

"Is it broke?" Roper asked.

"No," Clint said, "but see if you can move to the right a bit."

Clint hurried to the front of the team again, pulled them to the right as Roper got them going again. The wheel popped back up onto the road.

Roper was right. The road broadened after that. Clint was able to climb aboard next to him, and they drove to the mine, trailing the other two horses behind them.

When they got there, Roper reined in and set the brake. They both stepped down.

"So now what?" Roper said. "We don't want to start digging on somebody else's claim."

"Let's look around again," Clint said. "Maybe we'll find something that'll lead us to Pick-Axe."

Roper agreed and they started searching. Roper began looking on the outside while Clint went back inside and lit the lamp. He went in as far as he and Roper had gone before and continued. He came to a dead end. Presumably someone had dug that far and quit. He held the lamp aloft and studied the walls. There was no indication of color anywhere. He was about to turn and leave when he saw something leaning against the wall. He picked it up and carried it out.

"What've you got?" Roper asked, as he came out.

"What do you think?" Clint asked, holding up a sign that said FRIENDLY MINE.

Roper smiled.

"I think we've got it."

Chapter Fifteen

They spent time moving supplies from the buckboard to a camp near the mouth of the mine. They also made a point of posting the name Friendly Mine further down the road for anyone approaching to see.

Later that evening, as they sat at the campfire, Clint told Roper, "I went down another tunnel and found these." He showed Roper a bedroll and blanket.

"Pick-Axe must've been sleeping in there."

"But where is he now?"

"He better be alive," Roper said, "Or I'm going to find out why."

"I'm with you," Clint said. "I was thinking one of us could ride back to Nelson alone and look around, while the other one stays here and guards the claim."

"If we split up," Roper said, "we're putting both our lives at risk."

"That's true," Clint said, "but we also have Pick-Axe's life to think about."

"Okay, then I think I should go to Nelson, and you should stay here."

"Why you?"

"Two reasons," Roper said. "Nobody's going to want to try me on site like the Gunsmith."

"And?"

"And you know what you're doing here, I don't."

"But I can think of a third reason."

"What's that?"

"Pick-Axe knows you," Clint said. "If he's in hiding, he'll recognize you."

"There you go, then," Roper said. "I'll leave first thing in the morning."

"Whether you find Pick-Axe or not, it might be a good idea if you bring back some decent food."

"I'll take care of it," Roper said, looking at his plate. "More than just bacon and beans?"

"Please."

They both laughed and finished eating.

***

In the morning, after coffee, Roper saddled one of the extra horses.

"So what do I do, if the man who owns this horse comes along?" he asked.

"Tell him you bought it from me, and describe me," Clint said.

"And if he wants it back?"

"As far as he knows, you bought it," Clint said. "Make him pay you for it."

"And if he wants to know where you are?"

"Tell him," Clint said, "I'm up here, somewhere."

Roper mounted the horse.

"Let's hope he doesn't recognize me from following us."

"Or that he doesn't see you, at all."

Roper turned his horse and started off.

"Might be a good idea to see if there's any law in Nelson," Clint shouted.

Roper waved over his shoulder.

***

After Roper left, Clint went through the tunnels again. They were too smoothly worked, probably not by Pick-Axe Jones. And whoever dug them gave up and left without finding anything.

It was Pick-Axe who was stubborn enough to discover a vein, and realize he needed help and supplies to dig further.

But where the hell was Pick-Axe? Maybe Roper would find out.

Chapter Sixteen

When Roper rode into Nelson, the town seemed even busier than the day before. The street was easier to negotiate on horseback than in a buckboard, but there was still heavy traffic.

Roper figured the questions he had were better posed to Weber, the claims clerk. He made his way to the office, with many bumps along the way, which were accepted as the price to pay for making one's way down the street.

He dismounted and entered the office, decided to wait in line for his turn.

"Ah, you're back so soon," Weber said. "Did you find Pick-Axe?"

"No, but we found the mine," Roper said. "I was coming here to ask if you'd seen him. But I guess I've got my answer."

"Still no sign of him," Weber said. "But since his body hasn't turned up, I'd guess he's hiding out."

"Any idea where that would be?" Roper asked.

Weber shook his head.

"None, but there's plenty of hidey holes in these hills," the clerk said. "Mister, my line's getting pretty big."

"One more question," Roper said. "Is there any law in this town?"

"Funny you should ask . . ."

***

Following the clerk's directions, Roper found what looked like a hastily erected, makeshift sheriff's office. In truth, it looked more like an outhouse.

He dismounted and knocked on the door.

"Come!"

He entered and found himself in cramped quarters with a large man and a small desk. The man was grey-haired, big-bellied, wearing suspenders to hold up his trousers, which were straining with that belly, and losing.

"Help ya, friend?"

"I'm looking for the sheriff."

"Very funny," the man said. "Who sent ya here?"

"The claims clerk. He said you're the sheriff. That is, if your name is Nestor Teach."

"That's me," Teach said, "and yeah, they named me sheriff, but it was mostly a joke."

"A joke? Why?"

"Because I kept complaining that folks was stealing from me, and I wanted something done. So, they gave me the job, complete with a badge." He opened the desk drawer, took something out and tossed it on top. It landed with a clang. Roper saw a sheriff's badge three times the size of any he had seen before.

"Can ya see me wearin' this on my chest?" Teach asked.

"I guess not," Roper said. "But you do have the job officially, right?"

"Yeah, I guess I do."

He sat in the chair behind the desk, which almost gave beneath his weight.

"So I'm the law and this is my office," Teach said. "What can I do for you?"

"Do you know Pick-Axe Jones?"

"Everybody knows Pick-Axe," Teach said. "What's he done now?"

"I'm wondering if something's been done to him," Roper said. "I got to town yesterday, and I've been looking for him."

"What fer?"

"We're partners."

"In his new find?" Teach asked. "If it exists."

"Oh, it does," Roper said. "I found the mine. Now I need to find Pick-Axe."

"Well," Teach said, "he tends to hide out, because he's always fearin' somebody wants to steal his claim. He's kinda crazy that way."

"You mean the way you think people are stealing from you?" Roper asked.

"Listen," Teach said, "I ran a livery and things was always—okay, I see your point."

"So I assume you have no idea where he might be," Roper said.

"Naw, none. How'd you ever get mixed up with Pick-Axe?" the ersatz lawman asked.

"He did me a favor once, and we've been friends ever since," Roper said. "When he decided he needed a partner he could trust, he sent me a telegram."

"And you came?"

"He said he was sure he'd hit it this time."

"And he needed an investor, right?"

"A partner," Roper said.

"Well, good luck to you," the sheriff said, "Pick-Axe has a nose for color, but it never seems to run very deep."

"Well," Roper said, "I'm just warning you Sheriff. If anything's happened to him, I'm going to find out who's responsible."

"Good enough," the man said. "That'd keep me from havin' to do somethin'."

"And would you do somethin'," Roper asked.

"Well, I'd have to," Teach said. "After all, I'm the sheriff, ain't I?"

Chapter Seventeen

After Roper rode off, Clint poured himself another cup of coffee then carried it with him as he walked the area. He wanted to be sure there was no other access to the mine. He walked for several hundred yards either way and found no trails or footpaths. He looked up, couldn't really tell how far up the cliff went, but someone would have to drop down from above to get there.

Satisfied, he walked back to the camp and poured some more coffee. He took it into the mine with him . . .

***

Roper left the sheriff's office and headed for the general store he and Clint had bought their goods from. The store was busy, bustling with customers, but the clerk ignored them all and walked over to Roper.

"Can I help you and Mr. Adams with something?"

"Just a few things," Roper said. "Some meat, flour, vegetables, canned peaches—oh, a couple of bottles of whiskey. Just put it all in some gunny sacks. I'm riding."

"Right, sir."

"I'll wait outside."

The clerk nodded.

Roper stood out front, watching the people go by. He didn't see anyone giving any attention to the horse he was riding. He knew there was little chance of seeing Pick-Axe walk by, but he kept a sharp eye out anyway.

The clerk came out with two sacks and a bill Roper knew he had probably cut in half. He paid it and said thanks.

As Roper mounted up the clerk asked," Did you find Pick-Axe?"

"Not yet," Roper said. "Have you seen him?"

"Not lately."

"Do you know anyplace I might look?"

"You might check Trollop's Lane. He could be in one of their tents."

"At his age?"

"Those girls kinda like 'im," the clerk said. "They let 'im sleep there sometimes."

"Thanks. I'll give it a try."

***

Roper found Trollop's Lane, left his horse and continued on foot.

The girls were out in front of their tents with their hands up their skirts or down their bodices. Most of them looked worn out, which was why they were there and not set up in a "reputable" house.

"Nickel a poke, hon?" one asked him. "Better spent than a nickel a beer."

She went to lift her skirt even higher, but he stopped her.

"I'm not looking for a beer or a poke," he said. "I'm looking for a friend of mine."

"Hey, sweetie," she said, "we're all your friends, here."

"I'm sure you are," he said, "but the friend I'm, looking for is Pick-Axe Jones."

She dropped her skirt and lost her smile.

"Whatchoo want Pick-Axe for?"

"I'm his partner."

"Pick-Axe don't got no partners."

"He does now," Roper said. "In fact, he's got two."

"That right?"

"Yes, it is."

She looked him up and down.

"What's a high falutin' dandy like you got to do with Pick-Axe?" she asked.

"What makes you think I'm high faluting?" he asked.

She laughed.

"Even your dirty clothes is better than anything else I seen in weeks."

"What's your name, Miss?"

"They call me Old Poke 'round here," she said. "Wanna guess why?"

He didn't want to guess, but she looked over fifty.

"No, what's your name?" he asked.

"Betsy."

"Well, Betsy, I'm betting you're friends with Pick-Axe, and you're hiding him to keep him safe."

She narrowed her heavily made-up eyes.

"You really his partner?" she asked.

"And his friend," Roper said.

"Are there really people out to get him?"

"Now, that I don't know," Roper said, "and I don't think he knows for sure, either. But it's better to be on the safe side, don't you think?"

"Definitely," she said. "Okay, come with me, I'll take you to him."

"He's not in your tent?"

"I couldn't do business if he was, could I?"

She led him past most of the tents, some of which had girls out front, others had sounds coming from inside. Eventually, they reached a tent at the end of the row.

"This was Jenna's tent, but she ain't here no more," Betsy said. "You better wait here, 'cause we don't wanna spook him."

"I agree," Roper said. "Tell him Roper's here."

"Roper," she repeated. "I'll tell 'im."

She moved the flap aside and entered. Roper heard a low conversation, and the flap was flipped back again and the bandy-legged little Pick-Axe came charging out.

"Roper, goddamnit!" he shouted. "What the hell took ya so long?"

The little man gave the detective a bear hug.

"It doesn't really matter, Pick-Axe," he said. "I'm here, now."

***

After his inspection of the mine, Clint was convinced they were going to have to dig new tunnels. With just the three of them, it would take some time, but there was no way yet to be sure the strike would be large enough to bring in major materials. And for that they would need a major investor . . . but that could wait. First things first, a new tunnel.

Chapter Eighteen

Roper stepped into the tent with Pick-Axe while Betsy went back to work.

"When'd you get here?" Pick-Axe asked.

"Yesterday," Roper said. "We've been looking for you since then."

"Who's we?"

"Me and Clint Adams."

"The Gunsmith's here?"

"He's your other partner," Roper said.

"Three partners?"

Roper nodded.

"Three."

"I guess the Friendly Mine can support three part-ners," Pick-Axe said. "Does he know minin'?"

"Better than I do," Roper said.

"And nobody in their right minds would go up against us while we're partnered with the Gunsmith."

"Let's hope."

"That's good," Pick-Axe said. "I'm hidin' out from two jaspers named Tucker Samuels and Ike Milligan, who're tryin' to find our mine."

"Then we better get up there and keep it safe."

"So what are we waitin' for?" Pick-Axe asked. "Where's Adams?"

"He's at the mine," Roper said. "The claims agent gave us a map."

"Weber? He's not supposed to tell anybody."

"We convinced him. Do you have a horse?"

"I did when I got here," Pick-Axe said. "It's probably gone now."

"You can ride double with me," Roper said. "Come on, let's get out of town before somebody sees us."

They left the tent, walked to where Roper left his horse, pausing for Pick-Axe to say thanks and goodbye to Betsy.

"Bring your friend back here for some fun some time," she said.

"I'll do that."

Roper mounted up and pulled Pick-Axe up behind him.

"What's in these bags?" he asked.

"Some food."

"Good," Pick-Axe said, "I'm starvin'. Who's gonna do the cookin'?"

"We'll share the job," Roper said.

Pick-Axe slapped him on the back and said, "Like real partners."

Roper nodded and said, "Like real partners."

They rode out of town.

***

When they rode up the trail to the mine, Pick-Axe saw the sign.

"You found my sign," he said.

"Clint found it and put it up."

Pick-Axe cackled.

"The Friendly Mine is in business!" Pick-Axe exhorted, happily.

***

As they rode into camp, Clint walked to meet them.

"Glad you're back," he said. "Any trouble?"

"None."

Pick-Axe slipped down from behind Roper with a big smile on his face.

"Clint Adams! The Gunsmith! Who-eeee! My partner. Put 'er there." He stuck his hand out. Clint shook it.

"I just made a pot of coffee," Clint said. "Let's talk."

Sitting around the campfire, they found out that Pick-Axe had, indeed, been hiding out since he filed his claim.

"I didn't want anybody grabbin' me to make me tell 'em where it was."

"Good thinking, Pick-Axe," Roper said.

Pick-Axe looked at Clint.

Roper says you know minin'."

"I've been involved with a few."

"You've had time to look this over," Pick-Axe said. "Whataya think? Do we have somethin' here?"

"There's color here, that's for sure," Clint said, "but it'll take some digging to make sure."

"And three of us to do it!" Pick-Axe said.

"Well, we can make a dent. Have you panned in the stream?" Clint asked.

"Some," Pick-Axe said. "Found a taste, but it would take a helluva lot of panning to come up with anything worthwhile."

"Have you thought about building a sluice?" Clint asked.

"Not yet," Pick-Axe said. "Like you said, it's gonna take some diggin' to make sure."

"Right," Clint said.

"So when do we start?" Roper asked.

"Tomorrow," Clint said. "Let's get that horse unsaddled, and I'll take a look at what you brought in those sacks and make us a meal."

"Good-thinkin'," Pick-Axe said. "I'm starvin'."

Clint smiled.

"I'll see what I can do about that."

Chapter Nineteen

The clerk in the general store had packed a hunk of salted pork. Clint made a meal of it, along with potatoes and carrots.

"We're not going to eat like this often," Clint said, "so enjoy it."

"I am!" Pick-Axe said, enthusiastically.

"And how about this?" Roper asked, producing a bottle of whiskey.

"Sure," Clint said, "we should do all our drinking now, because there won't be any when the work starts."

"I agree," Roper said.

He took a drink and passed it to Clint, who preferred beer, so he took a short slug and passed it to Pick-Axe, who guzzled it.

"Easy!" Roper snapped. "We're sharing that."

Pick-Axe lowered the bottle, wiped his mouth on his sleeve, and passed the bottle back to Roper. One more drink and they went back to eating.

"The stream around the bend isn't deep enough to bathe in," Clint said, "but we can wash and do our laundry there."

"And pan for gold?" Roper asked.

"Later," Clint said. "I suggest first we go into the mine and start to work with pickaxes."

"I only have one," Pick-Axe said.

"We bought some more," Roper said. "Clint made sure we have enough supplies for the three of us."

When they finished eating, Clint took the plates and utensils to the stream to clean them, then took off his shirt and washed it, and himself.

"You fellas can use the stream to clean up," he said, returning to camp.

"I gotta wash?" Pick-Axe asked.

"Please," Roper said, "do it for us. You smell like a goat."

"Betsy didn't complain about how I smelt."

"Betsy smelled worse than you," Roper said.

"Betsy?" Clint asked.

"I'll tell you later," Roper said.

Roper waited for Pick-Axe to return, looking like an angry, wet cat, then went to the stream to wash himself. When he got back to the fire Clint had a fresh pot of coffee going. Eventually, they all had a cup, Roper and Pick-Axe sweetening theirs with a touch of whiskey.

"So what now?" Pick-Axe asked.

"You get a good night's sleep," Roper said. "Clint and I will split the watch."

"Suits me," Pick-Axe said. "I could use a good night's sleep. Tomorrow we get to work."

"Yes, we do," Roper said.

"And tomorrow we'll erect a tent, in case there's bad weather," Clint said.

"You have plans already," Pick-Axe said. "I like that."

"There's an extra bedroll over there," Roper said.

"Thanks."

Pick-Axe turned in while Clint and Roper remained seated at the fire.

"We finally get to work," Roper said. "I'm glad Pick-Axe is all right."

"So am I."

"Where will we start tomorrow?"

"Like I said," Clint replied, "we'll put up a tent. Then we'll go to work with the pickaxes and see what we can uncover."

"Where do we start?"

"The tunnels that are here look useless," Clint said. "They were dug with large tools, and nothing was found, so they were abandoned. But Pick-Axe did find a vein, so we'll start there."

"What if whoever dug those tunnels returns?" Roper asked.

"Doesn't matter," Clint said. "Pick-Axe filed his claim. This is his mine."

Roper dumped out the remains of his coffee.

"You mind taking the first watch?" he asked. "I'm a little bushed from riding."

"Go ahead, turn in," Clint said. "I'm good for four hours, or so."

"See you then," Roper said. "Good night."

Clint waved and tossed some more wood onto the fire.

Chapter Twenty

Roper woke Clint and Pick-Axe in the morning, with bacon in the pan.

"No eggs?" Pick-Axe asked.

"This is good enough," Clint said. "We have enough supplies for about a week of small meals. After that I'll go to town to pick up more."

"If you go to town, you'll have to watch your back," Roper said.

"I'm thinking most of the people in town are miners," Clint said. "The ones who aren't are gamblers, pickpockets, whores, or people building businesses—storekeepers, saloon owners—"

"—and there's a lawman, sort of," Roper said.

"That sheriff?" Pick-Axe said. "He's a joke."

"Some people think you're a joke," Roper said. "You're going to prove them wrong. That's what Sheriff Teach seems to want to do."

"I'll meet him," Clint said. "But I don't think anyone's going to be here looking for the Gunsmith when they can be looking for gold."

"Don't forget those two who were following us," Roper said. They had taken the time to tell Pick-Axe about them.

"I'm more worried about Samuels and Tucker. They like pickin' the bones of other people's claims."

"I think you're better off staying here." Roper said to both of them.

"It's not fair for you to go to town all the time," Clint said. "We're partners, remember?"

"If we go to town with the buckboard," Pick-Axe said, "we could load up on supplies so we'd only have to go once a month."

"That sounds good," Roper said.

"We'd have to back the buckboard down the road each time," Clint said.

"It'd work if Pick-Axe and I rode to town and loaded ourselves down with supplies," Roper said. "If one of us has to stay here alone it should be you. You'd do a better job of protecting the place."

"Maybe we should change the name to Gunsmith Mine," Pick-Axe said. "Then nobody'd come near us."

"No," Clint said, "that's announcing I'm here. That's just looking for trouble. At the end of the week, you two can saddle up and ride to town. Once you've bought the supplies, get right back here. The less time we spend in town, the better."

"Agreed," Roper said.

"As long as there's bacon, I'm happy," Pick-Axe said.

"I'm going to clean up here, and then we'll all go and look at that vein."

***

Armed with pickaxes, they entered the tunnel where Pick-Axe had found the vein.

"Let's get started," Clint said. "We'll stand far enough apart so we don't get tangled up and start digging. Pick-Axe, you start there, where you found this vein. Roper and I will work on either side of you. Maybe we can find a continuation of it."

They stood in front of the wall, approximately six feet between them, and started swinging their pickaxes. The air soon became rife with the sound of metal piercing rock, and flying chunks of rock. Afterwards, they used shovels to load the chunks of rock into the single wheelbarrow Clint and Roper had bought. They wheeled it outside, dumped it on the ground, and then two of them went back in to continue, while one stayed outside to go through the rubble.

It was decided that Clint could stay outside while Roper and a grumpy Pick-Axe went back inside.

"I should be the one lookin' for color," Pick-Axe complained, inside.

"I brought Clint to confirm that this strike is worth my investment," Roper said. "Once he's done that for me, you can take whatever job you want. For now, dig."

***

When Roper and Pick-Axe came back out, Clint had isolated several chunks of rock, and some smaller pieces.

"What've we got?" Roper said.

"Some definite color," Clint said.

"Color?" Pick-Axe asked, picking up a large chunk. "This piece alone could outfit us for a month."

"And tell everyone in town we've hit it," Clint said. "We don't want people to know that, do we?"

"No, we don't," Roper said, then looked at Pick-Axe. "Right?"

"Yeah," Pick-Axe said, dropping the rock, "right."

Roper grabbed the wheelbarrow and said to Pick-Axe, "Let's go in and fill this thing again."

"I can come in and help," Clint said, "or start supper."

"Why don't you start supper," Roper agreed. "Pick-Axe and I can fill the wheelbarrow, and check the haul."

"Fine."

Roper and Pick-Axe took the wheelbarrow into the tunnel, and Clint went to stoke the campfire.

Chapter Twenty-One

Clint made a meal of the pork that was left, some fresh vegetables, and biscuits. They passed around the half a bottle of whiskey that was left.

"We got some more good chunks out of that wall," Roper said. "Looks like a good strike to me."

"For it to be a strike, there's going to have to be more than just that one wall. Pick-Axe knows that," Clint said.

"Yeah, he's right," Pick-Axe said. "If this is a really hefty strike, it's gonna take a big company to get it all out."

"And would you sell?" Clint asked.

"Hell, no," Pick-Axe said, "but I'd take a partner who'd foot the bill."

"So would we all, I assume," Roper said.

"If that's what it takes to get it out of the ground," Clint said. "But we still have some work to do before we bring the big boys in."

They finished eating and, because there was still a bit of light, went back to the last rock pile they had taken out of the tunnel to have another look.

***

By that night they had gathered a small pile of what they had taken from the walls.

"This is going to be good, isn't it?" Roper asked Clint.

"Whataya askin' him for?" Pick-Axe asked. "I told you in a telegram we had somethin' here."

"And I told you, I brought Clint here to advise me."

"And be a partner, too," Pick-Axe said.

"You made it sound like we might have to fight to keep it," Roper said.

"And we still might."

"Pick-Axe," Clint said, "I didn't see a telegraph line when we rode in. How did you send Roper telegrams?"

"They got a telegraph in Linville," he said. "We write 'em out here, and then somebody rides to Linville with 'em."

"How often?"

"Coupla times a week," Pick-Axe said, "but if there's somethin' important, they take it right over. You got a telegram ya want sent?"

"Not yet," Clint said, "but when we've sussed out what we have here, we might."

"Just let me know," Pick-Axe said. "Okay if I turn in?"

"Go ahead," Clint said, "I'll clean up here."

"I'll take the first watch, tonight," Roper said to Clint as Pick-Axe walked away.

"Suits me," Clint said. "What about Pick-Axe? Are we going to have him stand watch, at some point?"

"I don't think so," Roper said. "He's not a young man. We'll let him get the rest he needs."

"That's okay with me," Clint said, standing up. "I'll wash these things and make some fresh coffee."

He went off to the stream.

***

When the coffee was ready Clint and Roper sat at the fire and had a cup.

"What do you think, Clint?" Roper asked. "I mean, for real."

"I think the vein he found is for real," Clint answered. "But before we can bring in big equipment, we'll need to find some other veins just like that one."

"So we'll be working for a while," Roper said. "You going to stick around?"

"I said I would," Clint said. "So I'll be here for a while—at least until we know for sure what we have."

"That's good," Roper said. "I'm not ready to bring anyone else in. I don't know who I'd trust."

"Don't worry about that, for now," Clint said. "We'll keep it the three of us." Clint looked over to where Pick-Axe was sleeping. "He doesn't seem real happy with me lately."

"He was real pleased when I first told him you were here," Roper said.

"That's when he was thinking about my gun," Clint said. "I don't think he likes being told what to do around here. He still thinks of it as his strike."

"He'll just have to get used to the three of us being equal partners."

"Maybe I'm too bossy," Clint admitted. "We should let him have more of a say in what we're doing."

"Hey," Roper said, "you're doing what I asked you to come here and do. Just leave Pick-Axe to me."

"I'll do that," Clint said. He emptied his cup and stood. "Tomorrow we should get the tent up. It's big enough to sleep two of us, while the third is on watch."

"I'll be ready for that come morning," Roper said. "Good night."

"See you in four hours."

Chapter Twenty-Two

In the morning, after breakfast, the three of them worked together erecting the tent. When they were done, they looked at the black clouds in the sky.

"Guess we got it up just in time," Clint said. "It's going to rain."

"It won't affect our work, will it?" Roper asked.

"Not particularly," Clint said, "but I'd like to see how rain will effect that stream."

"I guess we'll find that out soon enough."

Pick-Axe came over with a pick in his hands.

"We ready to go to work?"

"We are," Roper said.

He and Clint grabbed their picks and followed Pick-Axe into the tunnel.

The first time they came out with a full wheelbarrow the rain had started.

"Do you want to stay outside and go through all this?" Clint asked, dumping it on the ground.

"Afraid of the rain?" Pick-Axe asked.

"Hey, I'll do it if you don't want to," Clint said. "I thought you might like the change."

"No, I'll do it," Pick-Axe said, "I'll go get my hammer."

Clint went back inside with the empty wheelbarrow. He could hear Roper's pick digging into the wall. When he came around the corner, he saw Roper's bare torso gleaming with sweat.

"You take the next load out," Clint said, "the rain will do you good." He took off his shirt and tossed it aside, and reached for his pick.

"Where's Pick-Axe?" Roper asked.

"I thought he might like going through the load," Clint said. "He went and got his hammer."

"Yeah, he likes tapping those rocks, looking for color."

"And finding it," Clint said. "Every good chunk he finds brings him closer and closer to being right about a strike."

Roper and Clint stopped talking and started swinging their pickaxes, once again filling the wheelbarrow.

***

Roper wheeled the next batch out into the pouring rain and dumped it. Clint was right, standing there in the rain was refreshing. He stood there a moment, arms wide, basking in the cool wetness. Pick-Axe was there, his clothes soaking wet while he worked on the chunks.

"Oh, this is gonna be big!" he exclaimed to Roper. "Real big!"

"I hope you're right."

Roper turned to go back in, stopped short when he saw Clint coming out.

"I want to see what this rain is doing to the stream," he told Roper.

"Sure, go ahead. I'm going back in."

Clint walked around the bend and stopped short when he saw the stream. It had gone from a trickle to a driving stream, fed from a full-blown waterfall above. If the stream was this powerful to begin with, it would not have been a hard decision to build a sluice. However, when it stopped raining, it remained to be seen how long it would be before the flow became a trickle again.

He returned to the tunnel to work alongside Roper with his pickaxe.

***

Later in the day, Clint and Roper came out and found that the rain had let up, somewhat. Still, they chose to take a break and started for the tent. On the way there they found Pick-Axe trying to keep the fire going in the rain, to no avail.

"I was gonna cook, but the rain keeps puttin' the fire out," the little man said.

"Let's build it in the mine, in one of the dead-end tunnels," Clint suggested.

"That's a good idea," Roper said. He then turned to Pick-Axe and added, "But can you cook?"

"I been feedin' myself for years, ain't I?" Pick-Axe asked.

They watched the little man walk to the mine with an armful of dry firewood from inside the tent.

"I hope he's built like that just because he doesn't eat much," Clint said, "and not because of the way he cooks."

"You want to give him more to do," Roper reminded Clint.

"I know, but . . . ah, I guess we'll find out."

In spite of the fact that they were wet from the rain, they still walked to the now rushing stream to wash. When they returned, they donned some dry clothes, and decided to stay dry in the tent, rather than walk to the mine and watch Pick-Axe cook.

They listened to the rain wash off the top of the tent and used the handles of some shovels to poke the tent in places where the water was collecting. The last thing they needed was some holes in the tent.

"Well," Roper said, "two of us'll be dry in here tonight, while the other is on watch."

"You're taking the first watch, right?" Clint asked.

Roper gave him a look and said, "I thought you were."

Chapter Twenty-Three

Pick-Axe had turned the last bit of vegetables into a hot stew. He cooked it in a tunnel, and they ate it there while the rain continued.

"No more meat, no more vegetables," Pick-Axe said. "You know, one of you sharpshooters could go huntin' tomorrow."

"That'd keep us from having to go to town so soon," Roper said.

"I'll see if I can scare something up," Clint said.

"You'll see some deer up here," Pick-Axe said. "That'd do."

"That stream's going to be deep and cold for a while," Roper said. "We could butcher a deer and keep the meat in the stream."

"We could salt it," Clint said, "if we thought to buy salt."

"Put it on the list for next time," Roper said. "We've got flour."

"Not the same thing," Pick-Axe said.

"I meant somebody could whip up some biscuits for breakfast," Roper said.

"Ha, not me," Pick-Axe said. "This stew is all I can make."

"I'll go make some biscuits in the morning," Clint said. "Then I'll go hunting."

"In the rain?" Roper asked.

"It'll stop by mornin'," Pick-Axe said.

"You sure?" Roper asked.

"Positive," Pick-Axe said, "That's what it does up here."

"That's the plan, then," Clint said. "Breakfast and hunting."

"Pick-Axe and I will keep working the mine," Roper said.

"A few more days like today and we'd have enough to—" Pick-Axe started, but Roper cut him off.

"We're not going to use what we've got for drinks and a quick steak," Roper said. "We don't want anyone to know what we've got, yet. At least, not until we do."

"Whataya mean, what we got?" Pick-Axe asked. "We got a strike."

"We still need to figure out how big a strike, don't we?" Clint asked.

"I suppose," Pick-Axe said. "Seems I could buy a drink or two with no harm."

"You start flashing some cash around, there could be lots of trouble," Roper said. "Let's work together on this Pick-Axe, and keep it to ourselves."

"Yeah, yeah," Pick-Axe said. "Whatever you say."

They finished their meal, and Roper asked the older man, "You cooked, you want to clean up?"

"I'll clean my own mess," Pick-Axe said, sourly.

He took the pot outside and emptied it, then collected plates and utensils and took it all to the stream to clean.

"Coffee?" Clint asked Roper.

"We better leave that to Pick-Axe, as well," Roper said. "At least, until he mucks it up."

"I'm thinking I'll make the next trip into town," Clint said. "There's no point in me hiding up here. And if people know I'm around, it may lead to less trouble, not more."

"That's worth a try," Roper said. "It'd be nice not to have to set a watch every night."

"We might not get that far," Clint said, "but let's wait and see."

Pick-Axe returned and said, "The rain's let up. I'll make a pot of coffee in here, but we can sit outside and drink it."

"Sounds good," Clint said.

Pick-Axe grabbed the coffee pot and took it to the stream to fill it. When he finally had the coffee going, they each took a mug outside with them to drink. By then the rain had stopped completely.

In the absence of chairs, they managed to move three boulders around the campfire, but because the boulders were still wet, they took the coffee into the tent.

"If we got that buckboard turned around, we could take it to town and get some chairs and cots," Pick-Axe said.

"That might not be a bad idea," Clint said. "But even if we do that, I suggest only one of us go to town at a time. The other two can keep working, and also watch out for the place."

"We can back it down to the main road," Roper said. "Then drive it up again."

"I suggest when we get back, we leave it just off the main road and carry the supplies up. The chairs and cots won't be heavy, and the chow will be in sacks that are easy to carry," Clint pointed out.

"I'll go along with that," Roper said. "Using the buckboard, we could outfit for months."

"We better make a list of supplies for me to take with me," Clint said.

"You still want to go?" Roper asked.

"Yeah, I'll take my turn."

"I could come with ya and help ya load the buckboard," Pick-Axe offered.

"You can stay here and help unload the buckboard when he gets back."

"Aw, whatamatta, ya don't trust me?"

"Can you go to town and stay out of a saloon?" Roper asked.

"Sure I can," Pick-Axe said.

Clint and Roper looked at each other and Roper said, "Sure you can."

Chapter Twenty-Four

In the morning, Clint put off his hunting trip and they backed the buckboard down to the main road, then hooked up the team.

"When I get back, I'll come up and get you fellas to help me carry the supplies up," Clint said.

"Why don't we figure you'll get back before supper," Roper said.

"Who's cooking?" Clint asked.

"I am," Roper said.

"Okay, I'll be back for supper."

Clint climbed into the seat and started the team toward Nelson.

***

It was difficult getting the buckboard down the street to the general store. The rain had left deep puddles in the street, some thigh high. Clint had to be careful to keep the wheels from sinking in. Finally, he reined in the team in front of the general store.

"Mr. Adams," the clerk said, as he entered, "how nice to see you."

Clint felt this was more an announcement of his presence than a greeting. Other customers in the store turned to look at him.

"I've got a list, if you don't mind filling it," Clint said, and held it out to the clerk.

"Let me have a look," the man said.

"Got everything?" Clint asked.

"Pretty much," the man said. "This doesn't look so hard. How many chairs?"

"A couple would do," Clint answered. "And three cots, if you have them."

"I'll check out back," the clerk said. "Can you give me about half-an-hour?"

"I don't see why not," Clint said. "My buckboard's out front."

"I'll load whatever I've got for ya," the clerk said, "and keep an eye on it for ya. We don't want nothin' to go missin'."

"Thanks."

He was aware of the eyes on him as he left. There was a small saloon across the muddy street. He made it without sinking up to his knees.

Inside was crowded with mud-caked miners. There were no table games and no girls. Everyone was there to drink, and nothing else.

He went to the bar and made room for himself.

"Help ya?" the bartender asked.

"Beer."

"Sure."

He drew a beer and set it in front of Clint.

"Quite a mess here after the rain," Clint commented.

"It's a mess when it doesn't rain," the barkeep said. "New here?"

"Rode in a few days ago," Clint said.

"Lookin' for a job?"

"Not really," Clint said. "I've already got one."

"Too bad," the man said. "I could use some help here. Things in this town are gettin' crazy."

"Too much business?"

"There's never too much business," the bartender said. "Just not enough time in the day."

"There must be men looking for work," Clint said.

"Sure," the barkeep said, "miners, mostly. Nobody wants to tend bar in a boom. Too many drunk arguments and fights. Let me know if you want another."

"Thanks," Clint said, "but I just stopped in for one drink."

"Suit yourself."

The bartender went off down the bar to serve other customers.

Clint finished his beer with his back to the bar, looking the clientele over. In a corner he saw two men seated at a table and recognized them as the two who had been following them. Apparently, they had walked to town, or gotten a lift. He'd just as soon they didn't recognize him, so he finished his beer and left.

He stopped outside and wondered if the Krechmer and Buchanan were still looking for Pick-Axe. Neither he nor Roper had asked the old miner about them. He wondered what Pick-Axe owed them that they were so intent on collecting? He didn't know Pick-Axe as well as Roper did, but maybe the best thing to do was just ask him.

Before leaving the mine that morning, Roper had filled Clint in about meeting Sheriff Nestor Teach. Roper explained the man had gotten the job as sort of a joke, but Clint decided to stop in on the lawman anyway, to see if he knew anything about the two men.

Chapter Twenty-Five

As Clint entered the sheriff's small office, the law-man looked up from his little desk. The extra-large badge on his chest certainly did make the man look like something of a joke.

"Howdy," he said. "What can I do for you?"

"Sheriff Teach?"

"That's right."

"You talked to my partner a while ago," Clint said. "I'm Clint Adams."

Sheriff Teach stared at Clint for a moment, then said, "I was wonderin' if I was gonna meet you. What can I do for ya?"

"Do you know anything about two men in town who are looking for my other partner, Pick-Axe Jones?"

"Why do they want Jones?"

"That I don't know," Clint said. "I was hoping you did."

"Your partner musta told you how I became sheriff."

"He did," Clint said. "He also told me you want to do a good job."

"That's right, I do."

"Then you must be keeping track of strangers who come to town."

"That's a little hard to do in a boom town like this," Teach said.

"Well, these two fellas are in the saloon across the street," Clint said.

"Do they know you?" Teach asked. "Did they see you?"

"They do," Clint said. "But they didn't see me in the saloon. They looked like a couple of saddle tramps in their thirties, both wearing sidearms."

"I think I know who you mean," Sheriff Teach said. "They stopped in here when they got to town."

"Why'd they do that?"

"They wanted to tell me who they were," Teach said. "I give 'em credit for not laughing at me and my badge. And you didn't, either."

"The law's the law, Sheriff," Clint told him. "Did they tell you their names?"

"No," Teach said, "but they told me they're Pinkertons."

That Pinkertons were looking for Pick-Axe was interesting and concerning.

"Did they show you any identification to prove who they were?"

"No," Teach said.

"Did you believe them?"

"I didn't see any reason not to."

"And they told you they were looking for Pick-Axe Jones?" Clint asked.

"They did."

What did you tell them?"

"I told them I hadn't seen him in a while."

"How did they take that?"

"They said they wanted me to know they weren't leavin' town without findin' him."

"And did they say why?"

"I asked," Teach said. "They told me it wasn't my business."

"How did you respond?"

"I said I didn't want no trouble in town."

"And?"

"They said that was gonna be up to Pick-Axe," Teach said, "and any partners he might have."

"Well," Clint said, "I'm going to try to avoid any trouble."

"That's good news."

"But that might be up to them."

"I was afraid you was gonna say that."

***

Clint returned to the general store, saw the clerk loading supplies onto the buckboard. He looked over at the small saloon, saw some men coming out, but they weren't the two he was concerned with.

The clerk looked over at him as he approached.

"How'd we do?" Clint asked the man.

The clerk finished stowing what he'd been carrying and turned to reply.

"I got most of it," he said. "I even added some extras for ya. Just got in another hunk of pork. I figured you'd like to have it."

"Sure thing," Clint said. "The last one was good. Let me come in and settle up."

"I've got one more cot to load," the clerk said. "Come on in."

The clerk started inside. As Clint turned to follow, he saw the two men come out of the saloon. They didn't glance his way. He was tempted to go across the street and brace them but decided against it.

That would definitely not be a way of avoiding trouble, as he had promised the sheriff.

He went into the store.

Chapter Twenty-Six

As they entered, Clint saw a woman standing at the counter, waiting. She was a lovely brunette in her thirties, wearing a long, flowing purple dress, cinched at her trim waist to show that she had a full bosom.

"Miss Stockton, I'll be right with you," the clerk said. "I just have to finish with this gent."

"That's all right," Clint said. "Take care of the lady."

"That's very nice of you," she said to Clint.

"It's easy to be nice to such a lovely woman," Clint said.

"Oh, you're a charmer, I see," she said, smiling at him.

"Miss Stockton, this is Clint Adams," the clerk introduced.

Her eyebrows went up.

"What's the Gunsmith doing in Nelson?" she asked. "Don't tell me you're a miner, now."

"Just helping out a friend," Clint said.

"Well," she said, "while you're in town come and pay me a visit at The Palace."

"She owns the biggest saloon in town," the clerk told Clint.

"Well then, all the more reason to serve the lady first," Clint said.

"You heard the man," the clerk said. "What can I do for you?"

While the man took care of the lady, Clint walked to the door and watched the saloon batwings. He wanted to be sure the two men didn't spot him. He was dead serious when he told the sheriff he wanted to avoid trouble. But he would have liked to know if the men were truly Pinkerton Agents.

Miss Stockton appeared at the door next to him, holding a package wrapped in brown paper.

"If you come to the Palace, Mr. Adams," she said, "make sure to ask for Josephine. I'll make sure your first drink is on the house."

"I'll do that."

She looked at the buckboard and asked, "Is this yours?"

"It is."

"You must be serious about mining," she observed. "Where would this mine be?"

"Oh," he said, "it's out there."

She laughed.

"You're a careful man," she observed.

"Most of the time," he replied.

"If the Gunsmith is interested in mining," she said, "it must be a good strike. Keep me in mind if you decide you need an investor."

"I'll remember."

"You do that."

He watched the lady walk away, hips swinging very nicely. He wondered if she actually walked like that, or if I was for his benefit.

***

Clint drove the buckboard back to the mine. It was slow going with all the supplies. When he arrived, he put the brake on and walked up to fetch Roper and Pick-Axe.

"You made it," Roper said. "You want to eat before we unload?"

"I think we should unload before it gets dark."

"Let's get it going, then," Roper said. "I'll get Pick-Axe out of the mine and meet you at the buckboard."

"Fine by me," Clint said, and went back down the trail.

He had removed the three cots from the buckboard by the time Roper and Pick-Axe appeared.

"Did we get everything?" Roper asked.

"Everything and more," Clint said. "The clerk is a very generous man."

"That's because he knows he's dealing with the Gunsmith."

They each grabbed a cot and carried it up to the tent. Then they went back and did the same with chairs. That done, they started carrying sacks of supplies up the hill. It was dark by the time they brought the last load up. Most of the supplies were stowed in one of the dead-end tunnels. After that they sat in the tent and ate the meal Roper had prepared.

"Where's the meat?" Pick-Axe asked.

"Clint just got back with some. We'll have it tomorrow," Roper said.

"I can still do some hunting tomorrow," Clint said. "Then we'll have plenty of meat."

"Vegetable soup," Roper said, filling some bowls and passing them along.

"This is pretty good," Clint said, after a sip.

"Be better with meat," Pick-Axe grumbled.

"Oh, shut up and eat," Roper said, picking up his own bowl.

"I'm gonna eat outside," Pack-Axe said, and left the tent.

"Find out anything in town?" Roper asked.

"The population is swelling," Clint said. "The bartender in the small saloon across from the general store tried to hire me to help him tend bar."

"Were you tempted?"

"Very funny. I did see somebody familiar in the saloon?"

"Oh? Who was that?"

"Those two I caught following me—Krechmer and Buchanan."

"They were in Nelson?" Roper asked. "Do you think they saw you?"

"I don't think so," Clint said, "but they've got an eye out for Pick-Axe, according to the sheriff."

"You spoke with Teach?"

"I did," Clint said. "He told me those two came to see him, asking about Pick-Axe."

"Did they say why they wanted him?"

"No," Clint said, "they told the sheriff it wasn't his business, but they did say something very interesting."

"What was that?"

"They claim to be Pinkertons."

Chapter Twenty-Seven

Roper looked surprised.

"What would Pinkertons want with Pick-Axe?" the detective asked.

"Exactly what I was wondering."

"Maybe we should find that out from Pick-Axe," Roper suggested.

"You think he'll tell us?" Clint asked. "I get the feeling Pick-Axe keeps some things to himself."

"There's only one way to find out for damn sure," Roper said.

At that moment, Pick-Axe came back into the tent.

"This here is a time of day I like up here," he said. "Quiet, crisp . . . we got any whiskey left to sweeten the coffee?"

"No," Roper lied. "But we're glad you're back. We've got something to ask you."

"About what?"

Roper looked at Clint.

"Those two who followed us here from Linville," Clint said. "I disarmed them and asked them what they wanted."

"And?"

"They said you. You must know what they're looking for."

Pick-Axe looked puzzled. "What the hell did they want me for?"

"They said they've got to collect from you what's owed them," Clint said.

"What the hell do they say I owe them?" Pick-Axe asked, looking even more puzzled.

Clint was wondering if the look was an act?

"They didn't say," Roper replied. "We were hoping you'd tell us."

"How can I do that?" Pick-Axe asked. "I don't even know who they are. I toldja that. I only know about Samuels and Milligan, and they're bottom feeders."

"Well," Clint said, "according to the sheriff in town, Krechmer and Buchanan claim to be Pinkerton Agents."

"Teach said that?" Pick-Axe asked. "Did he get their names?"

"I didn't ask, and they didn't offer when I stopped them," Clint said, "and they didn't tell the sheriff. I left them on foot, but apparently, they made it to Nelson. I saw them in the saloon today."

"All the more reason for me not to go to town, then," Pick-Axe said. "There's four of 'em lookin' for me. I'll just stay up here and work."

"Well," Clint said, "with what I brought back today, none of us'll have to go to town for a while. Maybe they'll give up and be gone by then."

"Not if they're Pinkertons. They're a stubborn lot," Roper said, standing up. "I'm going to clean up."

"Are we goin' back into the mine?"

"No point tonight," Roper said. "We can get an early start in the morning, while Clint goes hunting."

"Suits me," Pick-Axe said.

"You two finish that pot of coffee and I'll make a fresh one when I get back."

As Roper left with plates and utensils to wash, Clint poured the last of the coffee into two mugs and handed one to Pick-Axe.

"Thanks," Pick-Axe said.

"You got anything you want to tell me while Roper's out there?"

"Like what?"

"Like who these two fellas who're looking for you might be? Pinkertons or not."

"I told you, I don't know," Pick-Axe said.

"Old partners?"

"I've had a few," the older man admitted, "but never hit it big with any. Can't see I owe anybody anythin'."

"Okay," Clint said, "if you say so."

"Gonna finish my coffee outside," Pick-Axe said, and left the tent.

Chapter Twenty-Eight

The next morning, Clint saddled one of the extra horses and went out looking for some meat. The two mounts he had taken from the men following them were inferior animals and made him miss his Tobiano.

While hunting, he kept his eye out for other mines, and other riders. The area near their Friendly Mine did not seem to be heavily worked. Pick-Axe had definitely been lucky to find this strike.

There didn't seem to be any other men within shouting distance. He would have liked to hunt above the mine, but he didn't trust the horse to make that climb, so he stuck to the area below.

He made a point of checking the buckboard to be sure it was still there, where he had left it. It didn't make sense to take it up to the mine, since they would only have to back it down again at some point.

He left the mine and the buckboard behind, riding down to flat ground where he thought he might pick up a trail. He finally caught one which, due to the size, made him think it was a stag. He started following the trail, and eventually sighted the animal a few hundred yards off. He managed to move closer without spooking it and saw that it was a 16-point red. It was a beautiful animal and, while it would be a shame to shoot it, they needed the meat in order to cut down on the number of trips back to town.

Clint raised his rifle and was about to fire when some movement caught his eye. He looked beyond the stag and saw two riders. He let the stag go, rather than attract attention.

He couldn't identify the men, but they could have been the two who were looking for Pick-Axe. And if so, they were getting too close to the mine. He turned his horse and headed back . . .

***

As he rode into camp, Roper was bringing the loaded wheelbarrow out of the mine.

"Where's the meat?" Roper asked.

"I had it in my sights, but let it go," Clint said.

"Why?"

"I saw two riders. Could've been the ones who are looking for Pick-Axe. I didn't want to attract their attention."

"You think they'll find us up here?"

"Maybe," Clint said. "They might see the buck-board."

"You want to bring it up here, again?"

"I think we should," Clint said. "If they don't see it, they might not find us."

"All right, then," Roper said. "Let's get it moved."

"We can use one of the team to pull it up," Clint said. "I just don't want it to be in plain sight."

"I'll get Pick-Axe. The three of us can move it."

"Okay, then," Clint said. "Let's get to it."

***

Between the three of them, they got the buckboard out of sight of the main road.

"We've got a tarp," Clint said. "Let's cover it."

The three of them draped the tarp over the buck-board.

"So you think these are the fellas lookin' for me?" Pick-Axe asked.

"They could be," Clint said. "I didn't get a good look."

"You want to head them off before they find us?" Roper asked.

"If we do that, they might think they're getting close," Clint said.

"They *are* gettin' close," Pick-Axe pointed out.

"Do you still have no idea who they could be?" Roper asked.

"I dunno."

Roper looked at Clint.

"Maybe we should take Pick-Axe out to have a look-see."

"That's an idea," Clint said. "I wish we had a spy glass or a pair of binoculars. We'll have to get him close enough to identify them."

"I should stay here and work the mine," Pick-Axe said.

"We'll make sure you see them, but they don't see you," Roper told him.

"Let's get it over with, then," Pick-Axe said, "so we can get back to work."

"Can you ride?" Clint asked Pick-Axe.

"Of course I can ride!" Pick-Axe snapped.

"Bareback?"

"Jesus!" the miner grumbled

"I'll give you one of the saddle mounts. I'll take one of the team."

"I'll saddle the other one for him," Roper said. "Are *you* going to be all right bareback?"

"I've ridden bareback more than you have," Clint said. "Let's get this done while they're still prowling around out there."

Chapter Twenty-Nine

Clint took Roper and Pick-Axe to the place where he had seen the stag, and the two riders.

"I don't see nobody," Pick-Axe grumbled.

"We'll find them," Clint said.

He rode toward where he had seen the stag, and Roper and Pick-Axe followed. They stopped on a high point and looked around. It was a panoramic view, and the two men were nowhere to be seen.

"Well, we didn't pass them, so they're not near the mine," Clint said.

"What about the sign?" Roper asked. "It announces the mine."

"You're right," Clint said. "We should take it down until we find out who those two are and what they want."

As they returned to the mine, they stopped at the base of the trail and looked up.

"It's amazing," Roper said. "From here you can't see a thing."

"Even when we get to the top of the trail, you can only see a stone wall until you walk around," Clint said. He looked at Pick-Axe. "Why aren't we seeing any other mines?"

"Most of the claims have been posted on the other side of town," Pick-Axe said.

"How did you find this one, to begin with?" Clint asked.

"I have a nose for it," Pick-Axe said. "And this time I think my luck is holdin'."

They rode up to the point where they had covered the buckboard.

"Still can't see a thing," Clint said.

"I'm going to pull up the sign," Roper said.

He did so, and carried it to the mine with him. He dismounted and put the sign inside the tent.

As Roper came back out Clint said, "We're going to have to keep a sharp eye out for those fellas. Pick-Axe, you'll take a watch. We'll do three hours each."

"That's fine with me," Pick-Axe said. "Whoever these guys are, I wanna see them comin'."

***

After a hard day's work the rest of the day, they gave Pick-Axe the last watch, so while he turned in, Clint and Roper sat at the fire.

"I've got an idea," Roper said.

"What is it?"

"You and I both know somebody at the Pinkertons," Roper answered. "Why don't we send a telegram and ask them if they've got men out here?"

"You think they'll tell us," Clint said. "They don't exactly like us."

"But whenever they need help, they call one of us," Roper said. "Let's call it pay back."

"I could send a telegram to Robert," Clint said. "He's the brother I get along best with."

"You'd be riding back to town so soon," Roper said, "but we could use some confirmation, if they really are Pinkertons."

"I'll ride back in tomorrow," Clint said. "It won't take as long on horseback as it did on the buckboard.

Clint had to admit he was curious about Josephine Stockton and her Palace. A visit to the saloon would be a way to spend time while he waited for a reply. Of course, that could take days, since the telegram would have to be sent from Linville.

"That sounds good," Roper said. "You could send the telegram, then one of us could go back in a few days and see if we got a reply."

"Probably me, since I'll be the one who sends it."

Clint decided to keep meeting Josephine Stockton to himself. The time to bring her up might be when they decided they needed investors.

***

The next morning Clint mounted up and rode to Nelson for the second day in a row.

Pick-Axe told him who the man was who took telegrams to Linville.

He found Ezra Kotzwinkle in The Palace, standing at the bar. He knew him from Pick-Axe's description of the man in his fifties with great big ears.

"Kotzwinkle?"

"That's right."

"I'm told you can go to Linville to send and pick up telegrams."

"That's right."

"Well, I've got one to send, and I want a reply."

"It'll cost ya," Kotzwinkle said, "for me to go with just one telegram."

"I'll pay," Clint said.

"When do ya want me ta go?" Kotzwinkle asked.

"As soon as I get it written," Clint said, then looked at the bartender. "You got a pencil and paper?"

"We don't deal with that," the bartender said.

"Is Miss Josephine here?"

The bartender straightened.

"You know Miss Stockton?"

"I do," Clint said. "Tell her I'm here."

The bartender came out from behind the bar and headed for the back of the big room. When he returned, Josephine was walking behind him. That day her dress was red.

"You here for your free drink?" she asked.

"That, and a pencil and paper. Your bartender tells me he doesn't deal in those."

"Wendell," she said to the barkeep, "give Mr. Adams a pencil and paper. And a beer. No charge."

"Yes, Ma'am."

The bartender put the drink on the bar, and then the paper and pencil.

"Thank you, Miss Stockton," Clint said.

"Come and see me in my office when you're finished," she said. "And call me Josephine."

"I'll do that, if you'll call me Clint."

"How nice," she said. "We're on a first name basis."

She turned and headed to the back. There weren't many customers at that time of the day, but they all watched her.

Clint leaned on the bar, wrote the telegram and gave it to Kotzwinkle.

"Don't come back without a reply," he told the man.

"Gonna cost extra for me to stay around."

"I'll pay it," Clint said. "You get going."

Kotzwinkle left The Palace, and Clint took his beer with him to Josephine's office.

Chapter Thirty-One

Ezra Kotzwinkle stopped at a large mine on the west outskirts of town and dismounted. The owner of the Holman Mine, a large, middle-aged man named Gus Holman, came walking over to him, after telling the rest of his men to keep working.

"What's this about, Ezra?" Holman asked.

"You said you wanted to know whenever anybody sends a telegram," Kotzwinkle said. "I thought you'd like to know about this one, right away."

"Why?"

Kotzwinkle held it out.

"This one is bein' sent by the Gunsmith," Kotzwinkle said.

"The hell you say!"

Holman snatched it from Kotzwinkle's hand and read it.

"Why the hell is he worried about Pinkertons?" the man asked.

"I don't kn—"

"I wasn't askin' you!" Holman said.

Kotzwinkle shut up.

"And what the hell is the Gunsmith doin' here in the first place?" Holman went on. "He's no miner." He looked at Kotzwinkle. "Is he?"

"Are you askin' me?"

"Of course I'm askin' you!"

"Well . . . there's word goin' around town that Adams and another man are partners with Pick-Axe Jones."

"I knew Jones was in town," Holman said, "but he never finds nothin'. Why would the Gunsmith be partnerin' with him?"

Kotzwinkle wasn't sure he was being asked a question, so he kept silent.

"He doesn't have a mine on this side of the El Dorado Mountains," Holman said. "What about the other?"

Kotzwinkle thought he should answer that one. "I dunno. There ain't really nothin' I know of on that side."

"I'm gonna have to find out," Holman said.

"Uh, there's another thing you should know."

"What's that?"

"There's two men in town looking for Jones," the messenger said.

"Then there's more I've got to find out."

"You want me to not send this telegram?"

"Hell, no," Holman said. "You don't send it, the Gunsmith will want to know why not." He handed the telegram back. "Send it, and when a reply comes in, bring it here first."

"Yes, sir."

Holman put his hand in his pocket and handed Kotzwinkle a wad of cash.

"And don't take your time doin' it."

"Yes, sir."

Holman watched the messenger mount up and ride off. Then he turned and walked toward his office, where he knew his foreman, Dack Simon, was.

Simon turned as his boss entered the cabin.

"What's up, boss?"

"You know if Samuels and Milligan are still in town?" Holman asked.

"Those two? They're always lookin' to pick somebody's bones."

"I want them."

"What for, boss?" Simon asked. "They ain't worth nothin'."

"I've got a job for them," Holman said. "And if they get robbed doin' it, I don't care."

Simon shrugged and said, "Okay, that makes sense. I'll find 'em."

"Bring 'em up here, and don't tell 'em what it's about," Holman ordered.

"That'll be easy," Dack Simon said. "I don't know what it's about."

***

Clint and Josephine did not take time to loll about in bed together. They both had business to tend to. But they each took pleasure in watching the other dress.

"Where are you off to now?" she asked, as he strapped on his gun.

"Back to work."

"Your mine?"

He smiled at her.

"You really can keep a secret, can't you?" she asked.

"Were you hoping for some pillow talk?" he asked.

It was her turn to smile.

"I got just what I wanted from between these pillows," she told him. "Feel free to come back any time."

"I'll do that, Josephine."

"I'll walk you out."

They left the back room and then the office. She walked him to the bar.

"Another beer before you go?" she asked.

"No, thanks," he said. "I better get going."

"When will you be back?"

"In a couple of days," he said. "I should have a reply to my telegram by then."

"I hope so."

She smiled at him and left. Outside, he mounted up and rode out of town and back to the Friendly Gold Mine.

***

While he was away Roper and Pick-Axe worked and talked.

"Do you still think we need the Gunsmith?" Pick-Axe asked his friend, at one point when they took a rest.

"More than ever, if Pinkertons are looking for you," Roper said.

"I don't believe those men are Pinkertons," Pick-Axe said.

"Then who are they?"

"I don't know," Pick-Axe said, "but there's no reason for Pinkertons to be lookin' for me."

"You keep saying," Roper said.

"And you don't believe me?" Pick-Axe asked. "Or Adams doesn't."

"I believe you Pick-Axe," Roper said. "I don't know what Clint believes."

"So you're still my partner?"

"I'm still your partner."

They went back to work.

Chapter Thirty-Two

Clint kept an eye out for the two men who claimed to be Pinkertons. He wanted to be sure he saw them before they saw him. He wasn't worried about the other two men, Samuels and Milligan, because according to Pick-Axe they were just bottom feeders. He doubted they'd have the courage to go against him or Roper.

Clint's horse was huffing and puffing by the time they reached the bottom of the trail to the mine. He doubted this animal would be much good as a team horse in the future. It might make sense to buy a couple of fresh mounts next time he went into town to collect his reply telegram.

He walked the horse carefully up the trail to the site of The Friendly Mine and saw his two partners standing there, bare-chested, sharing some water.

"You're back," Roper said.

"Grab a pick," Pick-Axe said.

"After I unsaddle the horse and rub him down," Clint said. "He's done in."

"Him?" Pick-Axe asked, looking at Roper.

"Clint tends to like horses better than people," Roper told him.

Pick-Axe shook his head and said, "And people think I'm crazy."

***

As Pick-Axe went into the mine and Clint unsaddled the horse, Roper came over.

"See anybody out there?" he asked.

"Not a soul."

"Get your telegram sent off?"

"Yes," Clint said. "I told the fellas to get an answer back here as soon as they could with no delay."

"See anybody else in town?"

"Yes, I did meet someone," he said. "I had to go to the Palace to find the messengers, and I met the owner."

"What's he like?"

"*She's* a businesswoman," Clint said. "She wanted to know if I was involved with a mine, and if I would keep her in mind if we needed investors."

"What'd you tell her?"

"Not a thing," Clint said, "beyond that I'd keep her in mind if it ever came to that."

"The Palace is the biggest business in town, isn't it?" Roper asked.

"It is."

"So she's probably got more money than anyone else," Roper said. "If we decided we do need an investor, she could be one."

Clint nodded.

"Maybe you should try getting close to her," Roper suggested.

"That's something else we could also keep in mind," Clint finished rubbing the horse down and tossed the brush aside. "Something else we might need down the line are some fresh horses."

"The team horses, you mean?"

"Yes," Clint said. "I don't think those two would-be Pinkertons are actively looking for the other two saddle horses."

"I hope Robert gets a reply off to you as soon as possible," Roper said. "I'd really like to know if we're dealing with Pinkertons."

"We'll find out soon enough," Clint said. "You want me to get in the mine with you, or cook?"

"We've got meat," Roper said, "so you might as well do the cooking."

"Is Pick-Axe going to complain?"

"You let me deal with Pick-Axe," Roper told him. "What we need right now is a real good meal."

"That's what you'll get, my friend."

***

In the mine, Pick-Axe put his tools aside and did some quick thinking while Clint and Roper were outside. He knew more about the two fellas following them than he let on. Pick-Axe Jones' past business relationships with people had not ended well. His last chance at a decent partnership was going to be with Talbot Roper. And because Roper brought him into it, also with Clint Adams. But if those men discovered that he wasn't telling the truth, that would be the end of it. And The Friendship Mine, Pick-Axe's last chance at any kind of success.

He was going to have to come up with a real good reason for why he didn't tell them the truth to start with. Of course, if the two men never caught up with them, he might not have to face that problem.

But he knew Clint Adams had sent a telegram to someone in the Pinkertons. He needed to come up with a plan before a reply came back.

Of course, they were still waiting for the mine to reveal a huge vein. Once that happened, he doubted Roper or Clint Adams would walk away.

He picked up his axe and drove it into the wall with all his might.

Chapter Thirty-Three

Dack Simon found Tucker Samuels and Ike Milligan at the smallest, cheapest saloon in town, the River Run, and told them his boss wanted to see them.

"About what?" Samuels asked. "He's already refused to hire us."

"Twice," Milligan added.

"Well," Simon said, "he's got a job for you now."

"Doin' what?" Samuels asked.

"That's for him to tell ya," Simon said.

The two men looked at each other and then Samuels said, "Let's go."

They followed Simon to the camp and into the cabin.

"You want me to stay, boss?" Simon asked.

"Yes, I do."

Dack Simon took up a stance near the door, hands folded across his chest.

"What's this about, Mr. Holman?" Samuels asked.

"Pick-Axe Jones," Holman said. "You know him?"

"We do," Samuels said.

"What do you know about him?" Holman asked.

"He's got a strike somewhere," Samuels said, "but we dunno where."

"And you're lookin' for it?"

"We are," Samuels said. "We bought 'im a drink one day, but then he went into hidin'."

"I think he's got at least one partner," Holman said, "maybe two."

"Who'd be partners with him?" Samuels asked.

"Clint Adams."

They both looked shocked, and Milligan said, "Jesus!"

"I want you to find them," Holman said.

"The Gunsmith?" Samuels asked. "You want us to go against the Gunsmith?"

"No," Holman said, "not go against him. Just find them and their mine."

"We've *been* lookin' for Pick-Axe's mine," Tucker said.

"In the right place?" Holman asked. "The other side of the El Dorados?"

"There ain't no strikes on the other side of town," Samuels said. "Nobody's over there."

"Pick-Axe is not on this side of town," Holman said. "That leaves the other side."

"You think Pick-Axe is good enough to find a strike over there?" Samuels asked.

"Look," Holman said. "He's an old miner who's always had an eye for color. He's just never had any luck.

The only reason somebody like the Gunsmith would partner with him is if they found somethin'." Holman took money from the top drawer of a desk. "I want you to search on the other side of town."

"Nobody works that side of town," Samuels said. "There's nobody there."

"Then nobody will get in your way." Holman walked to them and handed them each some money. "The same again when you find them."

Both men counted the money, then put it away.

"We'll look," Samuels said.

"Good," Holman said, "then go do it. And report to Dack."

The two men moved towards the door, and Dack Simon opened it for them. He closed it behind them and turned to face his boss.

"They'll probably take the money and run," the foreman said.

"They'll come back for the same amount again," Holman said.

"And when we find Pick-Axe Jones' mine, then what?" Simon asked.

"Then we'll take a look at it," Holman said, "and if it pans out, we'll add it to our claim."

"And what about the Gunsmith?" Dack Simon asked.

"We'll handle him when the time comes," Holman said.

Chapter Thirty-Four

As they came down from the Holman Mine, Milligan asked Samuels, "Why are we doin' this?"

"For money," Samuels said.

"Enough money to go against the Gunsmith?"

"You heard Holman," Samuels said. "Don't face him, just find them."

"So where do we start?" Milligan asked.

"There's two people who might know where he is," Samuels said, as they reached level ground. "Weber, the claims clerk, and Betsy, the whore."

"Pick-Axe and a whore?"

"A nickel a poke whore," Samuels said. "They're friends."

"And the clerk?" Milligan asked. "If he talks about claims, he'll lose his job."

"Only if somebody finds out," Samuels said.

"So we tell him if he tells us, nobody'll find out?" Milligan asked.

"No," Samuels said, "we tell 'im if he doesn't tell us, we'll let it be known that he talks."

"Oh," Milligan said, "so we lie."

Samuels smiled and said, "We lie."

***

Sitting around the fire having supper, Clint and Roper decided to question Pick-Axe again.

But first they discussed the meal.

"That clerk at the general store threw these wild turkeys in?" Roper asked.

"He told me he threw something extra in, but he didn't tell they were these birds."

"This one looks like it had a wing span of about forty-four inches," Pick-Axe said.

"This bird is delicious," Roper said. "You said 'these birds.' He gave us more than one?"

"Two," Clint said, "but I only cooked one tonight."

"Cook the other one tomorrow night," Pick-Axe said.

"I think I'll save it," Clint said. "Besides, there'll be plenty of this one left over."

"You know what'd go good with this?" Pick-Axe asked.

"What?" Clint asked.

"Whiskey."

"No," Clint said. "We'll make do with water from the cold stream."

"Pick-Axe," Roper said, changing the subject, "we want to talk about these men who are looking for you."

"Again?" the older man squawked. "I told you, I dunno."

"You know Samuels and Milligan, right?" Clint asked.

"Yeah, I do, but only around town," Pick-Axe said. "They're always lookin' for somebody to rob."

"So when they decided to buy you a drink . . ." Roper said.

". . . I got suspicious and went out the back door. I hid out until you found me at Betsy's."

Clint and Roper looked at each other.

"When do we find out if Krechmer and Buchanan are really Pinkertons?" Pick-Axe asked.

"I'm going to town tomorrow to check for a reply to my telegram," Clint said.

"And if you find out they're not Pinkertons?" the little miner asked.

"Then we're just going to have to find out who they are and exactly what they want," Clint said.

"And how you gonna do that?" Pick-Axe asked.

"We'll ask them," Clint said.

"Face-to-face?"

"Do you know of any other way?" Roper asked.

"Unless you just don't want to face them," Clint said.

"I ain't a brave man," Pick-Axe said, "but as long as I got the two of you beside me, I'll face anybody." He pointed. "Can I get another piece of that turkey?"

Chapter Thirty-Five

Samuels and Milligan came out to Betsy's tent and looked both ways.

"We didn't have to kill 'er," Milligan complained.

"She wasn't gonna talk," Samuels said.

"Maybe she didn't know where Pick-Axe is," Milligan pointed out.

"She knew," Samuels said. "She wasn't gonna say."

"Still—"

"Relax," Samuels hissed. "How did I know her neck would snap that easy? Come on, we better get out of here."

The other girls were all in their tents, entertaining from the sound of it. They hurried away before someone came out and saw them.

They left Trollop's Lane and headed for The Palace.

"Why the Palace?" Milligan asked.

"We been drinkin' there the last few days," Samuels said. "Now we can afford it. Tomorrow we'll go and see Weber and find out what he knows."

"Without killin' him," Milligan said.

"We'll see," Samuels said.

***

The two men claiming to be Pinkertons watched as Samuels and Milligan walked into The Palace.

"That's them," Pete Krechmer said. "The two the bartender told us do odd jobs."

"Odd jobs," Jelly Buchanan said, "like hirin' out to kill people."

"Well," Krechmer said, "we heard they'd been seen with Pick-Axe. Maybe it's time we found out whether or not they killed him. "If he's dead, there's no point in us stayin' around here."

"How do you wanna play it?" Jelly asked. "Brace 'em, follow em—"

"Let's keep an eye on 'em for a while," Krechmer said. "See where they lead us."

"I'm tired of this town," Jelly said.

"It'll dry up soon enough," Buchanan said. "That's how it goes with boomtowns."

"Can't be soon enough for me," Jelly said, standing. "I'm gonna get us two more beers."

"See if you can hear anythin' from them while you're at the bar," Buchanan said.

"Yeah, okay."

***

Clint sat watch while Roper and Pick-Axe turned in. Pick-Axe was not in the habit of cleaning himself well before turning in, so Clint liked waiting outside, on watch.

Clint felt that Roper wanted to believe Pick-Axe didn't know the two would-be Pinkertons. He hoped his friend was right, but if the miner did know the men, then he was lying to them. When you were partners with someone, they weren't supposed to lie to you. If Pick-Axe was lying, the outcome was going to be very bad.

One way or another, Clint hoped to know the next day.

***

Roper rousted Clint the following morning, having already prepared breakfast. Clint could smell the bacon and the coffee. As he approached the fire, Roper handed him a plate and mug. Across the fire, Pick-Axe was already eating.

"I'll ride into town and see if my reply came in," Clint said.

"Seems to me you're missin' a lot of the hard work, here," Pick-Axe said.

"You wanna eat your own cooking?" Roper asked.

Pick-Axe didn't answer.

"Do you not want me to get a reply, Pick-Axe?" Clint asked.

The little man stuffed his mouth, washed it down with coffee.

"Is there something you want to tell me before I go to town?"

The man put down his plate and cup, picked up his pick and went into the mine.

Clint looked at Roper.

"Don't mind him," Roper said. "He thinks you don't believe him."

"I don't," Clint said. "I know you do, but I don't." He put his empty plate and mug down and stood. "When I get back, it's all going to come out. Unless he talks to you."

"We'll see," Roper said.

Before Clint started for the horse—the second saddle mount he had taken from the two men—he said, "And see if you can get him to wash up before I get back."

***

Samuels and Milligan now had money for a hotel room, which they shared. It was the only one available, because someone had just checked out.

They left the hotel and went to a small cafe for breakfast.

"After this we'll go and see Weber at the claims office," Samuels said.

"To ask him a question," Milligan said, "not to kill 'im, right?"

"Of course," Samuels said, "he can't tell us where Pick-Axe's mine is if we kill 'im, can he?"

"I just wanna make sure," Milligan said.

"Come on," Samuels said, slapping his friend on the back, "let's eat."

***

When Clint rode into Nelson, he worked his way up the street and reined in his horse in front of the claim's office. As he dismounted, he saw movement inside. It looked like somebody was fighting. He hurried to the door and entered.

Two men turned quickly to look at him. They were holding the clerk, Weber, between them. When they saw Clint, they released Weber, threw him to the floor, and ran out a back door. Instead of chasing them, Clint reached down and helped Weber to his feet.

"Thanks," the man said, sitting heavily in a chair.

"What was that about?" Clint asked.

"They wanted to know where Pick-Axe's mine was," Weber said.

"Did you tell them?"

"I did not," Weber said. "Those two would kill 'im and steal his claim."

"Who are they?"

"Samuels and Milligan."

"Pick-Axe told me they were looking for him," Clint said. "Will they come back for you?"

"I'm sure they will," Weber said.

"Then I'll have to see that they don't," Clint said. "I'll talk to the sheriff."

"He's a little busy today," Weber said.

"With what?"

"Murder."

"Who was killed?"

"A whore on Trollop's Lane."

"Was it Betsy?"

Weber stared at him.

"How'd you know that?"

"She's probably the only other person who's seen Pick-Axe lately. They must have thought she knew where the claim is."

"Jesus," Weber said, "so they wouldn't've just give me a beatin', they woulda killed me."

"Do you have a gun?"

"Huh? Oh, yeah, in a drawer."

"Well, take it out of a drawer and keep it on you. I'll be back. Can you keep the door locked?"

"I shouldn't, during business hours."

"If anyone wants to file a claim, let them knock."

Weber nodded and said, "Okay."

Clint opened the door, then turned to face Weber.

"Where can I find Kotzwinkle?"

"Check the saloons," Weber said.

"The Palace?"

"Probably not."

"That's where I found him yesterday," Clint said.

"He was probably makin' some kind of delivery."

"Okay, thanks."

"You are comin' back, right?"

"Don't worry," Clint said. "I'll be back."

He left the office and headed for Sheriff Teach's office.

***

Pete Krechmer and Jelly Buchanan watched from an alley across the street.

"That was the Gunsmith," Jelly said. "He saved that clerk from those two."

"They killed that whore," Buchanan said. "Maybe they woulda killed that clerk."

"I don't think either one of them knows where Pick-Axe is," Krechmer said. "But Adams does."

"We can't follow him without bein' seen," Jelly said. "We'll have to finesse it. Wait for him up ahead, so he doesn't see us tailin' him."

"West of town?" Krechmer said.

"That's got to be where Pick-Axe's mine is," Jelly said.

"Could be a long wait," Krechmer said.

"We've been at this long, as it is," Jelly said.

Chapter Thirty-Six

As Clint entered the sheriff's office, the man looked up from his desk.

"I heard you had a murder last night," he said.

"How'd you hear that?"

"Weber."

Teach nodded.

"A whore named Betsy."

"She was a friend of Pick-Axe Jones," Clint said. "How'd she die?"

"Somebody broke her neck."

"Nobody heard or saw anything?" Clint asked.

"If they did, they ain't sayin'."

"What are you doing about it?"

"What can I do?" Teach said.

"Do you want some help?"

Teach perked up.

"Why would you do that?"

"I think whoever killed her was trying to find Pick-Axe's mine," Clint said. "I just caught Samuels and Tucker roughing Weber up for the same reason."

"You think they killed 'er?"

"I'm almost sure they did, but there are two other possibilities."

"Who?"

"The two men who told you they were Pinkertons."

"And are they?"

"I'm trying to find out," Clint said. "I sent a telegram to the Pinkertons. I'm hoping to get a reply today."

"Kotzwinkle?"

"Yes."

"You should know, he'll show that reply to anyone he thinks might be interested."

"That doesn't surprise me, in a place like this."

"I guess I'll have to go out and find Samuels and Tucker," Teach said.

"Are you up to it?" Clint asked.

"To tell you the truth, I ain't sure," Teach said.

"I'll go with you, then."

"You got the time?" the lawman asked.

"I've got nothing to do until I find Kotzwinkle," Clint told him.

"Then we better get goin'," Sheriff Teach said, standing.

He put on his hat and strapped on a gun, Clint wasn't sure it would even fire, if the need arose.

Chapter Thirty-Seven

They tried several saloons, but there was no sight of the two.

"The Palace?" Clint asked.

"That's the biggest, most expensive place in town," Teach said. "You think they'll be there?"

"Truthfully?" Clint said. "After I interrupted them in the claims office, I think they're going to be in hiding."

"We might as well give it a look then," Teach said. "Although I don't want to offend Miss Stockton."

"I don't think we have to worry about that," Clint said. "She's invited me to her place, any time."

"Then I guess we better do it," Teach said.

They walked to The Palace and stopped outside. Although it was early, the place was already open. They entered and approached the bar.

"Miss Stockton is in her office," the bartender told Clint.

"We're looking for somebody else," Clint said.

"Have you seen Samuels and Tucker?" Sheriff Teach asked.

"Those two? Huh-uh," he said. "When they come in, I toss them out, unless they show me money."

"Have you seen them today?" Teach asked.

"No."

Clint looked around the large interior. Only a few tables were occupied, but Samuels and Milligan weren't there, and neither were the two self-proclaimed Pinkertons. He also didn't see Ezra Kotzwinkle.

"Want a beer while you're here?" the bartender asked.

"Too early," Clint said. "Have you seen Ezra Kotzwinkle?"

"Don't think he's back from Linville yet," the barkeep said.

Teach gave Clint a look.

"Okay," Clint relented, "one beer."

***

Samuels and Milligan were across the street when Clint and Teach entered The Palace.

"Now's our chance," Samuels said.

"We ain't supposed to go against Adams," Milligan said.

"He saw us with Weber," Samuels said. "We gotta do somethin'."

"What about the lawman?"

"He ain't a real lawman," Samuels said. "Let's take 'em."

Milligan bit his lip, but in the end he said, "Yeah, okay . . ."

***

Clint and Teach had one beer, and then headed for the door. The lawman went out first and Clint heard a shot. He also heard the bullet strike and Teach staggered back. Clint caught him as he fell, then laid him down and ran outside, but it was too late. The shooters—he was sure it was Samuels and Milligan—were gone.

He ran back in and bent over the sheriff. He had his hand over the wound in the man's shoulder, blood streaming from between his fingers.

"You okay?" Clint asked him, eyeing the wound. "I'll get you to a doctor."

"Okay . . ."

He helped the man to his feet and said, "You'll just have to tell me where he is . . ."

***

Samuels and Milligan didn't stop running until they reached the Holman Mine.

Prior to their arrival, Dack Simon had told Holman about the dead whore.

"Who killed 'er?" the man asked.

"Everybody's pretty sure it was Samuels and Milligan," Simon said.

"Damn!" Holman said. "We didn't need that."

Just then a miner came running in.

"Hey, boss!" he shouted. "Samuels and Milligan just ran into camp."

Simon looked at Holman.

"Bring 'em in," Holman said.

Simon stepped outside, saw the two men in the center of the camp, looking around wildly.

"What'd you two do?" he demanded.

"We found Adams comin' out of The Palace," Milligan said.

"And?"

"Sam said to shoot at 'im, so we did," Milligan said. "Him and the sheriff."

"Are they dead?" Simon asked.

"Don't think so," Samuels said. "But the sheriff's hit."

"All right," Simon said, "the boss wants you."

He led the two men to the office and let them in.

"So?" Holman asked.

"They shot at Clint Adams and the sheriff," Simon informed him.

"Jesus!" Holman swore. "Kill 'em?"

"Hit the lawman," Simons said. "Not Adams."

"And you killed a whore!" Holman said.

"That was an accident," Milligan said. "Her neck just snapped."

"You two are useless," Holman said.

"Just give us the rest of our money, and we'll get outta town!" Milligan said.

"I'm gonna give you what you deserve," Holman said.

He opened the drawer of his desk, took out his gun and shot Milligan in the chest. At the same time the foreman took a gun from his belt and shot Samuels in the back. Both men fell to the floor, dead.

Holman put his gun back in the drawer.

"Get rid of them," he said.

Dack Simon nodded, put his gun back in his belt and headed for the door to get some men to move the bodies.

"And after you're done," Holman added, "bring Clint Adams to me."

"How am I supposed to get 'im to come here, boss?" Simon asked.

"How the hell do you think?" Holman said. "Ask him!"

Chapter Thirty-Eight

When Clint came out of the doctor's office, Dack Simon was there waiting.

"Mr. Adams?"

"That's right."

"My name's Dack Simon," the man said. "I'm fore-man of the Holman Mine."

"Congratulations."

"Mr. Holman would like to see you."

"About what?"

"Two men named Samuels and Tucker." Simon said.

"Where are they?"

"They're at the mine. Mr. Holman invites you to join him."

"Sure," Clint said. "Why not? Lead the way."

Simon did so. They made the walk in silence, and attracted attention as they entered the camp.

"The boss is in the office. This way."

Clint followed and preceded Simon as the man opened the door for him. When they entered, a man stood from behind a desk. He was tall, in good condition for what Clint figured was close to sixty.

"Mr. Adams. Thanks for comin'."

The two men shook hands.

"That's be all, Dack," Holman said.

Simon withdrew.

"Have a seat, please," Holman said.

Clint sat opposite the man.

"Your man said something about Samuels and Milligan."

"Yes," Holman said, "I understand they killed a whore, shot the sheriff, and shot at you. They're also looking for your partner, Pick-Axe Jones."

"That's all correct," Clint said. "Where are they."

"Dead," Holman. "How's the sheriff?"

"He'll be all right."

"I can arrange to have the bodies delivered to him."

"Do that," Clint said.

"Now, let's move on," Holman said. "I understand you have a mine on the other side of town."

"Who told you that?"

"The word is out," Holman said. "You, Jones, and another man are workin' a mine on the other side of the El Dorados, which everyone thought was dry."

"If everyone thinks that side of town is dry, why the interest?"

"Because," Holman said, "everyone also knows that this side of town is drying up."

"Is that so?"

"I'm willin' to invest in you and your partners," Holman said. "But first I need to see the mine."

"I haven't said there is a mine," Clint said.

"No, you haven't."

"Then we're done," Clint said. "I just want to see the bodies."

"Of course," Holman said, "but are you sure we can't talk about the mine?"

"What if I told you there's nothing to talk about?" Clint asked.

"I'm not sure I'd believe you," Holman said. "Just keep me in mind when it comes to investors."

"I'll keep the offer in mind," Clint said. "How's that suit you?"

"I guess that'll have to do."

Holman walked him to the door and waved the foreman, Dack Simon, over.

"Show Mr. Adams the bodies," Holman said, "and then back to town."

"Yes, sir." Simon turned to Clint. "This way, please."

Chapter Thirty-Nine

Clint stopped at the claim's office. Weber unlocked the door with his gun in hand.

"You won't need that," Clint told him.

"Why not?"

"They won't be back. They're dead."

"You saw them?" Weber asked.

"Yes."

Weber turned, walked to a cabinet and put the gun away.

"The sheriff was shot, but he'll be fine. I'm going back to the mine after I see Kotzwinkle."

"Kotzwinkle is back," Weber said. "He has your reply."

"Who will he show it to, first?" Clint asked.

"Probably Miss Stockton, and Mr. Holman," Weber said. "I don't know who else would be interested."

"And where's Kotzwinkle now?"

"There's a small café across the street," Weber said. "When he's in town, he has lunch there."

"I see."

"Will that be a problem for you?" Weber asked. "Him showing them your telegram?"

"Not really," Clint said. "It'll make them think they're on to something. That suits me."

"Then I can open?"

"You can," Clint said, "but I've been told claims are drying up. Is that true?"

"It is," Weber said. "I didn't file a new claim all day yesterday, and none this morning."

"So this strike is a bust?"

Weber pointed to the right. "This side of town is a bust." He pointed left. "If Pick-Axe is right, this side isn't."

"No one else on the other side?"

"Weber shook his head.

"Pick-Axe's claim is the only one on this side," Weber said, pointing. "Whether or not it's a strike, you know better than I do."

Clint turned toward the door.

"I'll find Kotzwinkle and then go back to the mine," Clint said. "Just between you and me, whether or not it's a strike is still in question. We have work to do."

"I won't say a word to anyone," Weber said.

"I know you won't," Clint said.

"Pick-Axe is my friend, and frankly," Weber said, "I'm more afraid of you than anyone."

"Then that'll do, Weber."

As Clint went out the door Weber shouted, "Thank you!"

***

Clint crossed the street to the little café and found Kotzwinkle sitting alone. The several other diners watched him walk across the floor.

"Do you have my reply?" he asked.

Kotzwinkle looked up at him.

"I do." He took it from his pocket and handed it over. Clint accepted it and sat down.

"Somethin' else?" Kotzwinkle asked.

"Who else have you shown this to?"

"No one," Kotzwinkle said. "It's your telegram."

"Let me put that another way," Clint said. "Who else besides Miss Stockton and Mr. Holman have you shown this to?"

Kotzwinkle looked afraid.

"It's all right," Clint said. "I just want to know who's read it before me."

"J-just them," he said.

Clint sat back in his chair, read the telegram, then refolded it and tucked it away. He stood up and called the waiter over. He gave him some money.

"This is for this gentleman's meal," he said. "The rest is for you."

"Yes, sir," the waiter said, "thank you, sir."

"Thank you," Kotzwinkle also said.

"Go ahead and finish your meal," Clint said, and left the café.

Outside he mounted up and rode to the doctor's office.

***

Sheriff Teach was sitting in the doctor's office, his left arm in a sling.

"Did you find them?" Teach asked.

"They're dead," Clint said.

"What about the other two you're lookin' for?" the lawman asked.

"I'll be taking care of them, too."

"Are they Pinkertons?"

Clint took the telegram from his pocket and handed it to Teach. The man read it and handed it back.

"I guess I better get back to my office, then," he said.

"You're better off going home for a while," Clint suggested.

Teach stood up.

"My office is where I live," he said.

Chapter Forty

Clint stopped at The Palace before leaving town. It was getting on into the afternoon, so the place was busier.

"Another beer?" the bartender asked as he approached the bar.

"No," Clint said. "Is Josephine in her office?"

"I haven't seen her today. She's probably still in her room."

"Which room would that be?" Clint asked.

The bartender looked confused.

"Upstairs," he said, "and I wouldn't go up there. She doesn't like anybody knocking on her door—especially in the morning."

"Got it. I just thought I'd say hello before I left town," Clint said.

"She should be down in a while, if ya wanna wait," the barkeep said.

"No, that's okay," Clint said. "Just tell her I dropped by."

"Sure."

Clint turned and left the saloon.

***

Jelly Buchanan said, "We been out here all mornin'. What if he's stayin' in town?"

"If he's workin' a mine, he ain't gonna waste time in town," Krechmer said.

"Then where is he, damn it?"

"Just keep your eyes on that trail," Krechmer told him.

"Jesus," Jelly said, "I can use a—wait a minute."

Jelly was sitting on a rock, and Krechmer was sitting with his back against it. Hurriedly, he got to his knees to take a look.

"That's him!" he hissed.

Jelly didn't move, so Krechmer grabbed his arm and yanked him down off the rock.

"Hey!"

"We'll let 'im go by, give 'im a head start, and then trail 'im."

"Not follow him?" Jelly asked. "Shouldn't we keep him in sight?"

"We don't want him seein' us," Krechmer said. "Just go and keep the horses quiet."

Jelly walked back to where they had left their mounts.

Krechmer watched from hiding as Clint Adams rode by. He recognized the horse as one he had taken from them. They'd had to buy new mounts and tack.

He watched until Adams was out of sight, then walked over to Jelly and the horses.

"Okay, let's trail 'im. He's gonna lead us to Pick-Axe and the mine."

"He better," Jelly said. "I'm tired of lookin'."

They mounted up and started their horses off at a walk.

***

When Clint rode back into camp Pick-Axe stuck his head in the mine and yelled, "He's back."

Roper came out of the mine and set his pick down. He and Pick-Axe waited for Clint to dismount.

"Any luck?" Roper asked.

"Lots. Let me unsaddle this horse and get some coffee and I'll tell you."

Roper and Pick-Axe went to the fire to wait for Clint. When he joined them, Roper handed him a mug of coffee.

"First off," Clint said, "Robert Pinkerton says he's got no men out this way."

"So we're not dealing with Pinks," Roper said. "That's good."

"The other two, Samuels and Tucker, are dead."

"You killed 'em?" Pick-Axe asked.

"No," Clint said, "that fella Holman did."

"Who's Holman?" Roper asked.

"Owner of the biggest mine on the other side of town," Pick-Axe said.

"Why'd he kill them?" Roper asked.

"I think it was to keep them quiet," Clint said. "They killed that whore, Betsy—"

"Betsy's dead?" Pick-Axe said.

"—and I caught them giving Weber a beating."

"What for?" Pick-Axe asked.

"It's pretty obvious they were looking for you," Clint said to Pick-Axe, "or us, or just this mine."

"If Holman's got a big mine, why's he want this one?" Roper asked.

"The word in town is that all the claims are drying up," Clint said.

"So Holman wants this one," Pick-Axe said. "That figures."

"Is that right?" Roper asked Clint.

Clint nodded.

"He offered to invest," Clint said.

"He ain't gonna invest," Pick-Axe said. "He's gonna wanna steal it. It's the only strike on this side of town."

"I also heard that," Clint said.

"If this is the only live claim on this side of town," Roper said, "we're going to have to be extra alert."

"Pick-Axe," Clint said, "those two fellas are not Pinkertons."

"That's good, right?"

"Depends," Clint said. "I think it's time for you to tell us who they are and what they want."

Chapter Forty-One

Pick-Axe looked at them nervously.

"Have you been lying to us, Pick-Axe?" Roper asked.

"Okay, look," Pick-Axe said, "this has a chance to be the biggest strike I ever hit."

"What's that got to do with two men looking for you?" Clint asked.

"I had two partners a few months back on a strike in California. Only it dried out before it panned out," Pick-Axe said.

"And?" Roper asked.

"And they invested just before it gave out," Pick-Axe said.

"And they want their money back," Clint said.

"How much?" Roper asked.

Pick-Axe hesitated, then said, "Ten thousand."

"Jesus, Pick-Axe!" Roper said. "You took off with ten thousand dollars?"

"I didn't take off," the smaller man said. "I invested it in the mine, and it dried up."

"Did you tell them that?" Clint asked.

"Yeah, but they didn't believe me," Pick-Axe said. "They think I just kept the money."

"Didn't you show them the operation you set up with their money?" Roper asked.

"I did," Pick-Axe said, "but they said they didn't see where their money had gone. They think there was no strike, and I pocketed their money."

"And?"

"They threatened to kill me if I didn't pay 'em back," the miner said. "I tol' them I would and then . . ."

". . . and *then* you lit out," Clint said.

"Well . . . yeah."

"With their money?" Clint asked.

"What was left of it."

"And it's gone?" Clint asked.

"Yeah."

"All of it?" Roper asked.

Pick-Axe nodded.

"And what about our investment, Pick-Axe?" Roper demanded.

"Roper, this strike is gonna pan out," Pick-Axe said. "I can feel it. You can see it."

"So far what we've found is a hint," Clint said. "We haven't hit a big vein, yet."

"We will," Pick-Axe said. "I guarantee it."

"The fact remains, you lied to us, Pick-Axe," Roper said. "You lied to me, your friend."

"Roper, I'm lettin' you in on a big one!"

Roper looked at Clint.

"Clint, I'm sorry I got you in on this," he said. "I believed everything he told me."

"There might still be a big strike here, Tal," Clint said.

"With everything you've heard in town, you still believe that?" Roper asked.

"We'll need an expert," Clint said, "a real expert, before we go any further."

"Where are we going to find one?" Roper asked. "Are you going to send back East for a geologist."

"We may already have one here," Clint said.

It took a moment, but Roper got it.

"You mean Holman?"

"Hey now wait a minute," Pick-Axe objected. "I ain't lettin' Holman in on this."

"He's the closest thing we've got to an expert," Clint said.

"That may be," Pick-Axe said, "but he's also a liar and a thief."

Clint looked at the man and asked, "You ever heard of the pot calling the kettle black?"

Pick-Axe looked confused.

Chapter Forty-Two

"Stop here," Pete Krechmer said.

Jelly reined in and looked around.

"I don't see nothin'," he said.

"That's the point," Krechmer said. "The trail stops."

"How can you tell on this hard ground?"

"Scratch marks from horseshoes," Krechmer said.

Jelly looked again.

"I see a lot of scratches," Jelly said.

"That's just it," Krechmer said. "There are fresh scratches back there, but none here." He dismounted and walked the area for a few seconds. Then he looked up.

Jelly looked and asked, "What're ya lookin' at?"

"Up there," Krechmer said. "There's somethin' up there."

"What?" Jelly squinted. "I don't see nothin'."

"There's a trail," Krechmer said. "Ain't been traveled much, but it has, recently."

Jelly scratched his head.

"I'm gonna hafta take your word for it," he said.

"Get off your horse," Krechmer said. "We'll take a look on foot." He handed Jelly his horse's reins. "Make sure they don't run off."

Krechmer waited for Jelly to secure the horses, and then join him at the base of the trail.

"That's hardly a trail," Jelly said.

"There's been some activity recently," Krechmer said. "Believe me, this is it. Just follow me and step where I step. Don't trip on or kick any rocks."

"Yeah, yeah . . ."

Krechmer started up the trail with Jelly close behind. An expert tracker, he could see all the indications of recent activity by men, horses, and wagons. He was annoyed with himself that he had not picked this up long ago.

Behind him Jelly stepped on a stone, almost twisted an ankle, and cursed.

"Quiet!" Krechmer hissed.

Eventually, they came to the empty buckboard.

"You was right!" Jelly hissed.

"Shut up! Of course I was right. I can smell a camp."

"I don't see nothin'."

"Don't worry, it's there," Krechmer said.

"Where?" Jelly whispered.

"Up ahead."

"There ain't nothin' there but a wall," Jelly complained.

At this point, if it wouldn't have made more noise than the man's mouth, Krechmer would have shot Jelly Buchanan just to shut him up.

***

"Wait!" Clint said.

"I'm tellin' ya—" Pick-Axe went on.

"Shut up, Pick-Axe!" Roper hissed. "What is it, Clint?"

"Somebody's coming up the trail."

"I don't hear nothin'," Pick-Axe said.

"They're on foot," Clint said. "Pick-Axe, get in the tent."

"What for?"

"I don't want anybody taking a potshot at you," Clint said. "At least, not until I decide if I want to or not."

"That ain't fun—" Pick-Axe stated, but Roper cut him off.

"Shut up and go!"

Grudgingly, Pick-Axe went into the tent. Roper ran over to where he had laid his gunbelt down and picked it up.

"How do you want to play this?" he asked, securing it around his waist.

"You hide just inside the mine," Clint said. "I'll be over here behind the tent. Let's not do anything until we see how many there are."

"Right."

***

Krechmer moved up the slope slowly, with Jelly close behind—sometimes too close. He put his left hand out to push him back a step or two. When they got to level ground, they saw only a rock wall.

"See?" Jelly said. "A wall."

"Quiet."

Krechmer looked both ways, then looked at the ground and decided they needed to go right. It looked like they'd be coming round a bend, and there was no telling what they were walking into.

He holstered his gun.

"Jelly, put your gun away."

"What? Why?"

"If we come around this corner with guns out, there's gonna be shootin'."

"So?"

"So there don't need to be," Krechmer said. "Let's just see what we're dealin' with first."

Jelly wasn't sure, but he slid the gun into his holster.

"Now just follow me," Krechmer said.

He moved forward, step-by-step, rounding the curve and eventually saw the entrance to the mine and the camp. At that point Clint Adams stepped out, his gun still in his holster.

"You fellas are back again?" Clint said. "What do you want, this time?"

"Would you believe," Krechmer said, "we want our horses back?"

Chapter Forty-Three

Roper stepped out of the mine, his gun also in his holster.

"What do you want?" Clint asked. "Really?"

"To talk," Krechmer said.

"Drop your guns to the ground and we'll talk," Clint said.

Krechmer hesitated, then slipped it from the holster and dropped it.

"You, too," Clint said to Jelly.

"Drop it, Jelly," Krechmer told him.

Grudgingly, he dropped it.

"Kick it away," Clint said

They both did. Roper came forward and picked both guns up.

"Okay, let's talk," Clint said.

"Can we do it over coffee?" Krechmer asked.

"Why not?" Clint asked and gestured for them to approach the fire.

The four of them crouched down and Clint poured four cups.

"What about Pick-Axe?" Krechmer asked. "Doesn't he want coffee?"

Clint hesitated, then called, "Come on out, Pick-Axe."

The little miner inched out of the tent, warily.

"They don't have any guns," Clint assured him. "Have some coffee."

Pick-Axe came forward and accepted a mug from Clint.

"Hey, Pick-Axe," Krechmer said.

"Pete."

Jelly glared at the miner but didn't say a word.

"You two told the sheriff you were Pinkertons," Clint said. "You're not."

"How do you know?" Krechmer asked.

Clint took the telegram from Robert Pinkerton and handed it to the man. He read it and handed it back.

"What he doesn't say is that we were Pinkertons," Krechmer said. "I guess we got fired when we became miners."

"Did that happen when you went into partnership with Pick-Axe?" Roper asked.

"Yes. Thinking back, we should've stayed Pinkertons. But to tell the truth, we were never comfortable there, and they weren't comfortable havin' us."

"Not everybody is," Clint said. "Pick-Axe told us about some money he owes you."

Krechmer looked surprised.

"He admitted it?" he asked.

"After a while," Clint said. "We didn't know in the beginning."

"We got no beef with you two," Krechmer said. "We know you're Adams. And you . . ." He looked at Roper.

"Talbot Roper."

Again, Krechmer was surprised.

"I know who you are."

"So now we all know each other," Roper said. "Are you here for trouble?"

"Hopefully, not," Krechmer said. "We only want our money back. We invested all we had with Pick-Axe. That was a big mistake."

"Yes, it was," Clint said, "but that's what happens when you invest. Sometimes it pans out, sometimes it doesn't."

"That's true," Krechmer said, "but we didn't even get a run for our money. Pick-Axe just lit out with it when the mine dried up."

"Before we even got started," Jelly added.

"By the way, I'm Pete Krechmer, this is Jelly Buchanan."

"We met on the trail," Clint reminded him. "I'm glad we have no beef."

"But we did have a beef with Pick-Axe," Krechmer said. "We want our money."

"That's between you and him," Roper said. "If this strike pans out, I suspect he'll have plenty of money to repay you with."

"And if your strike dries up?"

"Then we're in the same boat you're in," Clint said. "Making a bad investment."

"But from the looks of it, you got some play for your money," Krechmer said. "We never did."

"Well," Clint said, "you'll have to be more careful in the future with your investments."

Jelly's face turned red.

"Now wait a min—" he started.

"Quiet, Jelly!" Krechmer said.

"But—"

"Shut up!"

Krechmer was calm to that point, but now he seemed to get angry. Clint was unsure if it was with his partner or the situation.

"Okay," he said, "we've talked. You boys can go back to town and wait."

"Wait?" Krechmer asked.

"To see how our claim plays out."

"We waited long enough," Jelly said. "We want our money back."

"Like I said," Clint replied, "that's between you and Pick-Axe."

"Then we'll just take him and go," Krechmer said. "After we settle, we'll send him back."

Clint and Roper looked at Pick-Axe.

"Hey, now wait a minute—" Pick-Axe started.

"Don't worry, Pick-Axe," Roper said. "We're not giving you up, yet."

"Sorry," Clint said to Krechmer, "can't do it. You'll have to wait."

Krechmer looked at Jelly, and Clint was reading them both.

"Don't let him decide," he told Krechmer. "He'll make the wrong decision."

"Pete—" Jelly started.

"Never mind," Krechmer said. He looked at Roper. "Our guns?"

Roper looked at Clint.

"You took our horses once," Krechmer said, "we ain't leavin' without our guns."

"Let them have them," Clint said.

Roper took the two guns from his belt, unloaded them, then handed each man one. The two men exchanged them and holstered them.

"This ain't over, Pick-Axe," Krechmer said to the miner.

He turned and started away. Jelly followed. Clint followed them to the trail and watched them go down.

Chapter Forty-Four

Roper came up alongside Clint.

"What do you think?" he asked.

"I think they're going to be trouble."

"You shoulda killed 'em," Pick-Axe said from behind them.

They both turned and looked at him.

"That would've made it easy for you," Roper said. "You're going to have to settle with them."

"They wouldn've stood a chance," Pick-Axe argued.

"I don't kill unarmed men," Clint said, "and I don't kill men I don't have any reason to. I have no argument with them."

"But—"

"You're going to have to settle up with them," Roper said. "It's your problem."

Clint and Roper walked away, back to camp, leaving Pick-Axe looking down the trail forlornly.

"How do you want to play this?" Roper asked.

"That depends on how much more time you want to put into this, now that you know Pick-Axe has been lying."

"I'm stuck, Clint," Roper said, "but you can back out. I'll repay you."

"Don't be silly, Tal," Clint said. "I'm in, but I want to know what I'm in."

"So what do you want to do?"

"Those two are going to go back to town and tell people where we are," Clint said.

"Holman?"

"He'll hear, for sure," Clint said. "But I've got an idea."

"What is it?"

"We go to Holman," Clint said, "bring him and his expert up here, and find out what we've got. If it's a strike, we let him buy in. Pick-Axe can pay those two back, and we can decide what to do."

"You heard what Pick-Axe said about Holman."

"If Holman tries to steal this claim from us, he's not going to find it easy," Clint said. "But remember the pot and the kettle?"

"I know, I know," Roper said, as Pick-Axe came walking back to them. "But I knew what I was getting into, you didn't."

"Stop feeling guilty about getting me involved in a gold mine," Clint said. "We're going to make *something* out of this venture."

"Yeah, we are," Talbot Roper said, "we just don't know how much."

Chapter Forty-Five

It was agreed that Roper and Pick-Axe would remain on guard at the mine, while Clint rode over to the Holman Mine with their offer.

Clint had to leave the horse at the bottom of the hill and walk up to the Holman Mine. As he entered camp, he caught the attention of the workers who stopped to watch him approach the office.

The door opened before he got there and the foreman, Dack Simon, stepped out.

"Help ya, Adams?" he asked.

"I'm here to see your boss," Clint said.

"What about?"

"I've got an offer for him."

"Wait here." Simon went back into the building, but reappeared immediately. "Come on in."

He held the door to admit Clint. Holman was on his feet, waiting.

"What's on your mind, Adams?"

"We'd like to give you an opportunity to look our operation over."

"And?"

"If you think it's worth it, we'd take you on as a partner."

"Partner?" Holman asked. "How about I buy you out?"

"Why don't we wait and see what you think?" Clint countered.

Holman stared at Clint for a few moments, then said, "I'll come over with my geologist."

Clint thought the man might have one on call.

"When?" Clint asked.

"I've got to find my man," Holman said, "then we'll come over. Why, is there a hurry?"

"There might be some other offers," Clint told him.

"Like who? Josephine Stockton?"

"You know her?" Clint asked.

"I know most of the businesspeople in town," Holman said. "You've got to watch out for Stockton."

"Why's that?"

"She'll sweet talk you out of business," he said. "And if that doesn't work, she'll take it."

"Take it?"

Holman nodded.

"By force, if need be."

"Josephine Stockton?"

Holman nodded.

"You telling me she's interested?" he asked.

"Yeah, she's interested."

"Why would she be more interested now?"

Clint told Holman how Pick-Axe Jones owed two men from a past encounter, and how they found the mine.

"I sent them back to town," Clint said.

"And word's gettin' around," Simon said.

"That's what I figure," Clint said.

"Okay," Holman said, "wait here. I'll get my man and we'll come with you." He looked at Simon. "Get some men."

"Yessir." Simon left the building.

"More men?" Clint asked.

"Like I said," Holman replied. "Stockton might want to take it." He headed for the door. "Wait right here."

Holman left the building and Clint heard him yelling for someone. When he came back, he had five men with him, including Dack Simon.

"Adams, this is Hanz Mohlzberg, my geologist."

"Glad to know you," Clint said. The man nodded.

Mohlzberg was a barrel-chested German who wore little wire-framed glasses.

"Let's go," Holman said. "Let's get some horses."

Chapter Forty-Six

They heard shots as they approached the mine.

Lots of shots.

"I told you," Holman said. "Stockton."

"You think she sent men to take the mine?" Clint asked.

"She wouldn't send 'em," Holman said. "She'd lead 'em."

Roper and Pick-Axe are alone up there," Clint said.

He kicked his horse into a frenzied run, and the others follow.

***

The lead flying into camp surprised Roper and Pick-Axe.

"Grab your rifle!" Roper yelled.

"I ain't no good with a gun!" Pick-Axe complained. "Where's Adams when we need 'im."

"Just grab a rifle and start shooting!"

Roper overturned the wheelbarrow and they took cover behind it. Bullets started pinging off the surface, the sound ringing out . . .

***

"There!" Clint said, pointing.

They could see at least half a dozen men at the top of the trail, firing around the bend. The only thing saving Roper and Pick-Axe was that the men couldn't get a clear shot from where they were. They were going to have to move ahead, round the bend, as soon as they got the nerve.

"Come on!" Clint called.

He rode hard for the base of the trail, where he dismounted and started to fire up the hill. Holman and his men followed. Mohlzberg stayed behind with the horses. The horses belonging to the shooters had already scattered.

As Clint, Holman and his men advanced, firing as they went, the men at the top turned and changed the direction of their shots. But they were at a disadvantage, caught between the camp and the trail, in a crossfire. They began to spin and fall, and before long the remaining men threw down their guns and raised their hands.

Clint came to the top of the trail, with Holman and his men behind him, and walked toward the surrendering men . . .

. . . and woman.

"Josephine," he said.

Dressed like a man, despite the way she filled out her clothes, she was easily mistaken for a man.

"Clint," she said. "Holman."

"What the hell are you doing?" Clint asked.

"Well," she said, "it didn't seem to me you were going to invite me in, so I thought I'd just . . . take it."

"How do you even know there's something to take?"

"Two men came into my place and started talking about your mine. They even said where it was. So . . ." She shrugged.

Holman's men started taking Josephine's men down the trail.

"Let's go, Josephine," Clint said. "You're going to the sheriff."

"That idiot?"

Clint smiled.

"That idiot's going to put you in a cell."

As Holman's foreman led her away, she called back, "Will you come and visit me?"

"Not likely!" Clint called.

Clint turned and saw Roper and Pick-Axe approaching him.

"You fellas okay?"

"We are, now!" Pick-Axe said.

***

Clint, Roper, Pick-Axe and Holman waited in the tent, drinking coffee laced with whiskey.

"This Mohlzberg, he's going to be able to tell something right away?"

"He's got ways," Holman said. "I don't want to waste a lot of time."

"This is a strike," Pick-Axe said, "a big strike. I can tell."

"I've got a theory about you, Pick-Axe," Holman said.

"What? That I'm an old fool? Like everybody else thinks?"

"No," Holman said, "I think you've got a nose for this business. But you enjoy the chase more than the strike."

"What?"

"Don't you see? You never stay around long enough to find the big one."

"Well," Pick-Axe said, "I'm stayin' now, and this is a big one."

"No," Mohlzberg said, "it is not."

They all turned and looked at the man who just entered the tent. He was holding a glass test tube.

"There is color here," the German said. "You vill haf to dig deep, if you vant it."

"Why wouldn't we dig deep?" Pick-Axe asked.

"It vould be a lot of work for some return," Mohlzberg said, "but certainly not vat I would call a strike."

The five men looked at each other.

"Goddamnit!" Pick-Axe said.

"I'll dig," Holman said. "I'm here, my men are here. I'll dig until I hear of a strike somewhere else." He looked at Clint, Roper and Pick-Axe. "I'll buy any of you out. Pick-Axe, if you want, you can work for me."

"Work here?"

"No," Holman said, "go find me another strike somewhere." He touched his nose. "Follow your nose."

"And if I do that?"

"I'll buy you out here."

"You can have my third," Clint said.

"And mine," Roper said.

"You can have mine," Pick-Axe said, "but I'll work for ya."

Holman looked at Dack Simon and said, "Draw up the papers."

"Yessir."

Then he looked at Mohlzberg and said, "Show me."

He followed the geologist out of the tent.

"Why's he doing this?" Roper asked.

"Because for him, it's worth it," Clint said. "For us it'd be too much work."

"So where are you going from here?"

"New Mexico," Clint said, "to get my horse. Where are you going?"

"To Denver," Roper said, "back to the work I know. I've had my fill of mining."

"So have I."

Roper held his cup out and said, "I haven't had my fill of that though."

Clint tilted the whiskey bottle and topped him off.

Upcoming New Release

THE GUNSMITH

CHEAP WHISKEY AND SAD WOMEN
BOOK 481

A saloon owner wants Clint to endorse his own private label of whiskey. He wants to put Clint's picture on the label and call it Gunsmith Whiskey. The WCTU—Women Christian Temperance Union—is against it...

For more information
visit: www.SpeakingVolumes.us

Now Available!

THE GUNSMITH
BOOKS 430 – 479

**For more information
visit: www.SpeakingVolumes.us**

Now Available!

THE GUNSMITH GIANT SERIES

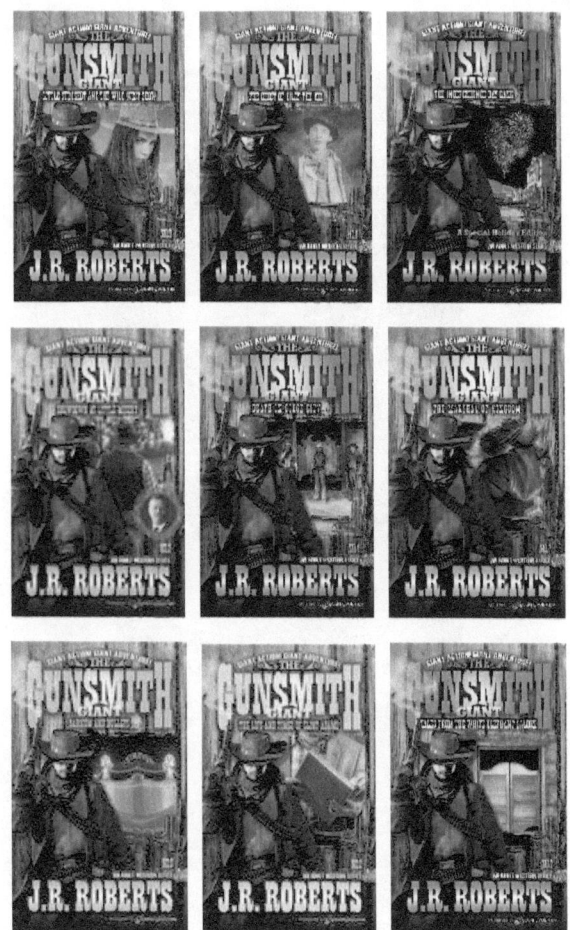

Now Available!

AWARD-WINNING AUTHOR
ROBERT J. RANDISI (J.R. ROBERTS)

www.ingramcontent.com/pod-product-compliance
Lightning Source LLC
Chambersburg PA
CBHW021701260626
47154CB00022B/1309